I0654062

SPECTRUM OF LIES

BREAK A CURSE

RED MOON

OUTLANDERS OF THE MULTIVERSE COLLECTION

BY D.N. LEO

Narrative Land Publishing
Narrativeland.com

PART ONE

CHAPTER 1

"**O**rla!" Lorcan's scream seemed muffled by the fog as he saw her turn around to look at him with tears streaming down her face. And then she vanished into the thick mist.

What have I done? Lorcan asked himself, not expecting an answer. He stared into the emptiness and felt the vibration of the energy Orla had left behind. A blizzard. It felt like thousands of blades of ice were slashing at his skin.

Was this the end of Orla and him?

The Irish countryside blurred in front of him. This was the riverbank where they had become childhood sweethearts. But it had now become where their relationship ended. "Orla!" he called out again but expected no response as he remembered the vision of her blending into the smoky air of the mysterious river.

Why? Lorcan struggled harder to free himself, but his legs felt like they weighed a ton. His body didn't obey him. He did his best to turn around.

Behind him, the woman pulled the upper half of her dress up to cover her breasts. She pulled her long, flaming red hair back to reveal her perfect face and the flawless skin of her delicate neck. Her striking blue eyes pierced at Lorcan at the same time as a smug smile crossed her face.

"What did you do to me?" Lorcan asked while summoning all of his leftover power to move.

"Nothing you didn't want." She smiled again.

Lorcan thought he had gotten things under control. Bricius, a nasty sorcerer he had fought and killed during his last mission, had cursed his parents before he died. Although Lorcan had no idea how to break a curse, he had traveled back to Ireland alone, without Orla. They had fought so hard to be together, free from the curse her family here had bound them with, and he couldn't take a chance she would get tangled up in that mess again.

He had landed at the riverbank after exiting the portal of the Daimon Gate. But before he even had a chance to congratulate himself for successfully sneaking back to Ireland without Orla, he saw her. He should have known. She always seemed to know where he was. She smiled at him. It was the usual Orla smile. But there was something more to it.

Lust.

It didn't surprise him. They had run away from this place to be able to love each other freely and be together. And now, here they were, back together—and at the riverbank. Love was the only thing he had in his mind, and he was sure it was in hers as well.

She's irresistible, he had thought and then grabbed at her. He kissed her as he always had. But this time, it was different. As soon as he touched her, the air around him seemed to turn into a vacuum of some kind, and he was 'sucked' into her. That was the last thing he remembered, and that had been the last moment when he'd been able to control his movement.

The eyes of the woman staring up at him now were not Orla's. His arms were moving up and down her body, pulling up her dress. His mouth ravished hers. But it wasn't he who controlled the actions. His body seemed glued to hers. His mind was numb. He heard himself screaming on the inside for it to stop.

He was watching himself from outside his body. *Bloody hell!* He was having sex with this strange woman, and he couldn't do a thing stop it.

Then he heard a daunting sound.

"Lorcan!"

Orla's shaky voice stabbed into his heart. She had followed him back to Ireland after all. He couldn't turned around himself—the woman had to push him. Nothing hurt him more than the look on Orla's face.

She walked away from him and vanished into the fog.

CHAPTER 2

"**W**ho are you?" Lorcan asked the woman.

"I am the one you were in love with. She was just a convenient replacement."

"What?"

"All the time you were looking at me at the riverbank, you think I didn't know? You were watching me from the bush. You were there for *me*. Remember? It was *me* that you wanted. You were going to build me a castle."

Lorcan stared at the woman for a long moment, then nodded. "It was you, my childhood fantasy. All those years, I was in love with you . . ." Lorcan whispered as he gazed at the woman.

The woman teared up. "You remember?"

"Yes, of course." He tried to walk toward her but failed. He raised his arms to reach out to her, to embrace her. But his body didn't cooperate. "I remember," he said. "Let me hold you again."

The woman smiled and waved her hand.

Lorcan felt as if a thousand tons of heavy air had been lifted from him. His body and his mind worked again, and the thought that instantly crossed his mind was rage. It gathered inside him. "Never ever call Orla names!" He grunted out the words and glared at the woman, a wave of electric current shooting from his eyes. It struck the woman, lifting her off the ground and throwing her rolling onto the wet grass. "No one can replace her."

Lorcan charged at the woman, hauling her up. "Who are you, and what do you want from me?" But his hands gripped a pile of clothes. The woman had vanished like smoke. A wedge of icy air hit him from behind. Lorcan fell, rolling on the ground. Behind him stood a woman who looked the same as

9

the woman he'd just attacked—he recognised her eyes—but this time, she was twenty feet tall, and her face was ancient, marked with scars and veins. She raised sharp claws and made a sweeping gesture. Lorcan's body was swiped off the grass, spun up in the air, and smashed down in the middle of the river like a rag doll.

From beneath the icy water, he saw the woman smirk. Her arm reached out, keeping Lorcan submerged. He knew shooting an electric wave from under the water wasn't wise. He kicked hard but couldn't free himself. He was running out of air when the woman started laughing. Lorcan reached for his gun and found it had slipped out and sunk to the bottom of the river.

Then the woman pulled him up to the surface. "You could have lived happily forever after with your bitch Orla out there. Why bring her back and take what's mine?"

Lorcan gasped for air. "I came back to visit my family. It has nothing to do with Orla. She doesn't care what's yours."

The woman let out a demonic laugh. "You fool. You think she follows you back here for love? Do you know who she is? Do you know what she would

10

become in two weeks?" The woman dunked him in the water and pulled him back up again.

"I know who she is . . ." He gasped for more air.

"You know nothing. In two weeks, I will get what I want. If only she hadn't shown her face."

"I'll take her out of here. There's nothing here that we want."

"It's too late. They'll never let her leave this time." She brushed her bony fingers across his face. "What a pity! I thought I could have a taste of you. See what all the fuss was about. See what it's like to have the man she'd left everything for."

"She didn't leave here because of me. She left because she didn't want to be surrounded by people like you."

The woman laughed. "She will have to live with it now. Or should I say, *die* with it now!"

"If you want to kill me, do it. She wouldn't have come back if not for me."

"You'd die for her. How sweet! Let's do it."

Lorcan tried to yank her hands from around his neck, but they were clenched as tight as a vice.

"Were you really the girl at the riverbank?"

"You can't play the same trick on me twice, Lorcan. But yes, I was." Then she plunged his head under the water again. This time, it was for a very long time. He struggled for a while, and then he let go. He let his mind and his body flow free with the current. He hung on to nothing.

She pulled him up again. "She thinks she's protected here. Big mistake. She'll die painfully. And you'll have to help me to do that . . ."

Lorcan opened his eyes and shot the electric wave at the woman as soon as she lifted him out of the water. She screamed and released him. He swam to the riverbank while the woman burned like a torch.

As soon as he hit the riverbank, he ran as fast as he could. The woman whirled around and swung her arms. A wedge of icy air rushed over her, and the fire died out. Lorcan charged ahead. A few more feet and he would reach the bush and find a place to hide. But the woman clawed at him from behind with arms that had stretched out at him like two snakes. Blood spurted from his back as he fell to the ground. The woman flipped him around. *She's going to gut me,* Lorcan thought.

"I'll skin you and show whatever's left of you to the bitch Orla. See if she can handle this. See if she bursts into flame. No one is going to take what's mine."

The woman raised her talons. Lorcan used what energy he had left to shoot out the electric currents, but they died out like pitiful sparks before they reached her. Her claws came at him menacingly.

Suddenly the haunting sound of a lullaby wafted out from the other side of the bush. It was his mother's lullaby.

The woman screamed, "No!"

The song hovered in the air, and the soothing melody kept coming. The woman yelled again, "No! Stop!" She covered her ears with her hands and spun around. But it didn't seem to help. Her body burst into flames again. This time, the fire was stronger and harsher. She raced into the woods, her haunting moans trailing behind her as she ran.

The bush returned to its eerie quietness. Lorcan thought he heard the woods sigh. Blood poured from the wound from his back and weakened him by the second. He needed to pass out in order to heal his wounds, but it wasn't wise to do it here. If wild animals, creatures from hell, or that mysterious woman came back while he was lying somewhere in a ditch shivering from fever, it would be the end of him.

He pulled himself up to his feet and darted in the direction of the place he had once called home. Trees and the darkness surrounded him, disorienting him. He kept running, and the pounding of his heart cause even more blood to gush from his wounds. He had run this very route with his mother once when he was six. He had killed for the very first time here to protect his mother. He couldn't see much, but the haunting lullaby guided him. He followed the song. The music floated on the wind, seemingly coming out of nowhere.

He didn't mean to throw a tantrum whenever his mother sang this lullaby. He actually enjoyed it, but he thought a boy shouldn't like a lullaby. Or at least so he thought when he was six. She had stopped singing it for a long time. So many things had happened between that time and now, and he had stopped talking to his mother. The words of the lullaby came to mind, and suddenly he began to mumble the lyrics under its breath. The song of a little lost boy finding his way home.

He hadn't been a little boy when he'd left. He hadn't been lost. He loved his parents, and he knew he had their unconditional love. But something in him told him that he didn't belong in the peaceful Irish countryside. And then he'd found Orla. It was like finding his other half. And he knew then where his life was meant to be.

It was Orla who stood between him and his parents. He had never told her he'd chosen her over his family because it was a wound that had never healed in his soul, and there was no point in her carrying the baggage.

But now it seemed he had lost from both ends.

Just before the last drop of energy drained out of him, he saw the gate of his family's mansion. The door swung open before he reached it, and once inside, he fell into the arms of his parents and his sister.

He had made it home.

CHAPTER 3

Cold reality slapped at Orla's face as she ran aimlessly into the woods. She had left Lorcan at the riverbank with a strange woman. The scene of him holding the woman had ripped at her heart. She knew infidelity wasn't in Lorcan's blood, but she had underestimated how much it would hurt her to see him with another woman.

They had been through so many life and death situations. She recalled the many times she'd held him in her arms, knowing that life was drifting away from him and having no clue how she'd ever survive if he died. But nothing compared to this!

The pain knocked the wits out of her. She ran until her legs began to cramp and her breath hissed in and out of her lungs in painful spurts. She finally collapsed onto her knees. When she looked up, the entrance of a graveyard loomed over her. She pulled herself up to her feet, using the low stone wall for support. She looked over the wall at the moss-covered gravestones, letting the misty fog and slight breeze soothe her broken heart.

The magic that her family possessed made it easy to keep private cemeteries looking scary enough so that they were left alone. She knew that the fog wasn't the ghosts of the dead, aimlessly wandering around their burial places. She finally caught her breath enough to stand up straight and limp her way down the gravel walkway toward the back of the cemetery where her aunt's grave was.

Aunt Siobhan had been more than just her mother's sister. Since her parents had died when she was five, she had known Aunt Siobhan as her mother. She had been a mentor in more than just magic, and she had been the one to give Orla hope that love was still attainable.

She set her feet on the familiar path, letting them carry her to the very back of the cemetery where the wild trees and grasses of the Irish moors began to creep up over the walls. She loved that her aunt's grave was here. Siobhan had been more of an elemental, using nature itself in her magic and spells. Now it almost seemed like nature was coming to be a part of her again, even after she was dead. As the fog rolled back, the grave marker came into view through the mist. The wild grasses and moss had started to grow up the stone, and Orla did her best to peel them off with her bare hands. She knelt down in front of it when she'd finished clearing the vegetation.

Then she thought of Lorcan again, and the fresh wound opened. She let her tears flow freely now, watering the grass at the foot of the stone.

"Don't go watering the weeds! There's no point in me coming here every month to do the weeding if you're just going to encourage them to grow."

Orla's head jerked up, her heart racing as she turned around slowly. "Maeve! Oh boy, am I glad to see you!"

Maeve was Siobhan's daughter, and she and Orla had grown up together. Maeve smiled at her and helped her up for a welcome hug. Orla stumbled a little, as her legs had cramped up from kneeling down on the uneven paving stones.

"You should be glad it's me instead of someone else. There's a bit of a storm brewing. You'll be in trouble if they find you. You should stop by Mom's old house. It's empty and abandoned. You should be safe there for a while." Orla gave Maeve a hug and an extra squeeze.

"Thank you. Your psychic read has gotten much better over the years, I can tell."

The smile faded from Maeve's face. "I saw clouds, Orla. You didn't come back by yourself. A storm is following you, and this one is bad."

The pain had crept up on Orla again, and she teared up.

"It's him, isn't it?" Maeve asked.

Orla nodded and wiped her tears away.

"It's poor timing, Orla. Couldn't you have waited another two weeks to return?"

"What's the difference?"

"It's a full moon in two weeks, and Bradan will become the leader of the clan."

"Bradan?"

"Your distant cousin, Orla!"

Orla squinted. "Oh . . . oh . . . Who would have thought!" Orla exclaimed remembering the skinny, freckle-faced, red-haired boy that all the girls, including her, had picked on all the time. She cleared her throat. "So I guess he'd grown up a strong candidate for the leadership. But what does that have to do with my timing? I broke my promise with the ancestors. If they catch me, they'll burn me. And so what?"

"The position has always been yours until replaced by the newly chosen. So that's Bradan, and that will be in two weeks' time. Unless you really want to . . ."

"Hell no."

"If you don't want to take up that post with the clan, why come back now?"

Orla had no answer. She had left and had been gone for years. She'd sworn to never set foot in the village again. There had been many times she'd wanted to come back to visit Aunt Siobhan's grave and Maeve, but her haunting past had put her off. She couldn't live the emotionless life of black magic again.

And then came Lorcan. He had found her in the city after she'd run off for a few years. He'd left everything behind for her. Before she knew it, he had become a part of her life that was more important than anything else.

Then came this trip. Bricius had cursed his parents, and he'd had to come back to Ireland. He'd thought he could get away and leave Orla in Eudaiz. But she had followed him anyway. Ciaran had helped her, warning that her trip was against Lorcan's wishes. Her thought circled back to the scene at the riverbank. *Who was that woman?* she wondered.

"Orla!" Maeve called out.

"Huh?"

"What's the matter?"

The image of Maeve became blurry and flickering in front of Orla. *Oh crap!* Someone was using black magic on her.

CHAPTER 4

Orla swayed and tried to hang on to her consciousness. She should have known. What had she expected, coming back to the land of black magic, to the place where she'd grown up, where she had been trained and where she owed a debt?

She hadn't been practicing for years. Her knees buckled. She heard Maeve calling out for her and felt her hands on her shoulders. Her best friend could help. Aunt Siobhan was a white witch, and Maeve practised white magic. She wasn't part of the clan, and she was Orla's only hope. They had been communicating in their psychic minds for years, and she was sure her trip to the Daimon Gate wouldn't have broken their psychic communication channel.

"Help me!" Orla managed. She couldn't get many words past her lips, but she remembered mind reading was one of Maeve rare gifts. "Read me!" She reached her hands out and tried her best to clear her mind to communicate with Maeve. She felt Maeve's cool hands grabbing hers and a slight energy passing through her body. The warmth of the energy helped.

"Concentrate," Orla told herself, willing the muddy clouds from her mind. The scene of Lorcan and the woman at the riverbank flashed back into Orla's mind. As much as it hurt her, she forced herself to analyze the situation. Someone was using the black magic on her. Someone was trying to break up her relationship with Lorcan. Someone wanted her to resent him.

A sharp pain pierced through her brain, and Orla suddenly slumped to the ground, breathing heavily.

"Hold on, Orla, keep thinking. I'm with you," said Maeve.

The resentment grew quickly into hatred. Orla could read her mind like an outsider and could see her conscious mind was leaving her. "I want to hate Lorcan." The words were demonic. It came deep from her throat and from her soul.

"What are you talking about? You confuse me, Orla. Your mind is confusing. I can't get hold of it," Maeve cried in a panic.

Orla's head was throbbing. She was losing it. She gasped for air as tears streamed down her face. She summoned a last thread of hope. "Someone is trying to get me to curse Lorcan from hatred. Please don't let me . . ." She groaned in pain, breathing heavily and trying to shake the thought from her head, but the mud was getting in again. The clarity was leaving her. She thought of Lorcan again, which was probably not a good idea. She almost lost control of her mind.

"Black magic!" she whispered. Lack of practice was doing her no good at the moment.

"Don't let go, Orla. I've got you."

She heard Maeve's voice in the distance. Everything seemed blurry.

"Tell Lorcan I love him."

"No, you tell him yourself."

Blood trickled from her nose. "Lorcan betrayed me. He kissed that woman." The words coming out of her mouth weren't hers. Tear streamed down her face, and her self-awareness slipped in and out. "He kissed that woman. I . . ."

"Don't say that, Orla. You'll put a curse on him, and you're going to regret it. You're strong. You can control it," Maeve's voice echoed in from a distance.

Orla cried. Her mind wandered back to the apartment she and Lorcan shared in London. She walked into the living room. She could sense him. She could hear his laughter. She saw him fumbling with the coffee machine, trying to fix it so the sharp lever wouldn't cut her next time she used it. He smiled at her. She loved his beautiful blue eyes. She smiled back .

The bed had blankets on it, and the pictures of them on the wall were hanging askew. Some of their pictures had fallen to the floor. Glass was everywhere. "Someone broke into our apartment! That woman—she stole him from me!" Orla yelled.

"You're hallucinating, Orla. Concentrate. Don't let it get to you. I can't help you if you let it take over your mind."

Her heart lurched painfully in her chest, thinking about how happy she'd been in London with Lorcan, but now all that filled her mind was Lorcan and that other woman. Rage began to build inside her, and she was beginning to feel a dull throb behind her eyes.

"It hurt!" Orla whispered.

"I know. Come on, Orla, look at me."

"It hurt so much," she said out loud, and once again, the words weren't hers. "I hate Lorcan. He'll pay for what he did to me."

"Stop, Orla. Stop!"

She heard Maeve yelling at her, but she couldn't stop. She drifted back to the apartment again. Looking at a picture of the two of them together was the last straw. She reached up and yanked the picture off the wall so forcefully that the nail behind it bent. As she threw it onto the ground, breaking the glass in the frame, the pain in her head grew worse. She tore through the room, ripping everything that reminded her of Lorcan off the walls.

At the graveyard, she could see herself hitting the stone marker and ripping weeds out. She saw Maeve trying to hold on to her. But then her mind slipped off again. The world became empty, and she burned with a desire to destroy.

"He has to pay for what he did to me . . ." She began to chant a curse while tears streamed down her face. The last drop of self-awareness was slipping out of her. Images of Lorcan flashed on and off at the back of her mind. "I curse . . ." She hadn't finished when a hard blow on the head put her out.

CHAPTER 5

A warm cloth wiped at his back with gentle strokes, as soothing as the hand holding it. Someone was checking his shoulders. Lorcan breathed in as much as he could, he wanted to capture and hold on to the familiar smell from the fresh bed linens and the comfortable pillow his head was resting on—it was the fresh floral scent from the pouch his mother always put into the linen cabinet. She said it was her secret formula, a scent that was unique and memorable to this family. He knew it now—it was the scent of home. He realized now how much he had missed it over the years.

"Good morning!" the voice sang like gentle and merry bell. Lorcan was facing the wall, but he didn't have to turn around to recognize his little sister's voice, Keeva Brody. He turned around to smile at her as he always did, but instead, his jaw dropped and he was speechless. Sitting at his bed side was a stunning woman with magnificent hair and twinkling eyes that he just knew smiled all the time and made people feel warm and happy.

Keeva rubbed at her face and frowned.

"I'm sorry, I thought you were my little sister! Would you like to go out on a date with me?" He grinned.

Keeva laughed and poked his side. Lorcan grabbed his sister and, in one swift move, pulled her onto the bed. He covered her with the blanket and held her tightly. He could feel her body vibrate with laughter. It had been five years since he'd last seen her in London after she had sneaked to the city to visit him. Regardless of her beauty and how much she had grown up since, she was still his little sister.

"You got a boyfriend yet?"

"Huh?"

"I would be surprised if you aren't seeing someone."

"Don't play, big brother. You should have seen yourself last night and the mess you put yourself in."

"Were Mother and Father really mad at me?"

"That was the first time they'd seen you in more than a decade. I'd definitely be mad if I were them. But surprisingly, they didn't say much. Just took care of you. It seemed like they had known you were coming home."

Keeva sat up in the bed. Lorcan sat up as well and glanced around his room. Everything was intact—just as it had been when he'd left. The decoration was from his teens, and he didn't think the comic book hero collection that he'd thought was so cool then was too cool now. "Where are they?"

"Father went into town. He'll be home shortly. Mother is . . . well . . . in the kitchen."

Lorcan raised an eyebrow. He didn't remember his mother cooking. There were more people who worked in the house than the family members themselves. Reading his mind, Keeva smiled. "She's supervising the chef. She's new, and Mother said she wanted to make something special for you."

Lorcan nodded as he hopped off the bed. His head was throbbing with a headache, and the purpose of this trip had come back to him.

"Before you go anywhere, Lorcan, can you explain to me how the wounds on your back healed in just a couple of hours? When I first looked at them, I didn't think you'd survive. If Father hadn't stopped me, I would have taken you to the hospital, or at least called a doctor."

"Father stopped you from calling the doctor?"

Keeva nodded. "He said you'd heal. I don't know what the hell he meant—he didn't explain."

Lorcan frowned. *Father knew about his werefox ability?*

"Lorcan?" Keeva called out, waiting for an answer.

"I just found out about it recently. I'll tell you later. Right now, I've got to see Mother."

Keeva rolled her eyes and followed her brother to the kitchen. As they walked down the stairs and turned into a long corridor, the smile faded from Keeva's face. "What is that, Keeva?"

"Something's wrong." Her voice shook, and the blood drained out of her face.

Seeing Keeva's eyes darken, Lorcan darted toward the kitchen.

Keeva had never been an 'official' psychic. He'd always thought of it as an unfortunate gift that she had. She could sense death. The first incident was her pony. She sensed his death just before they had found him attacked and gutted by the wolves. The second was his parrot, who had died for no apparent reason. The third was the death of an old man who'd called himself a shaman. He lived in the woods and had nothing to do with the village and befriended no one.

The grand country kitchen greeted them with the inviting aroma of a freshly baked lemon and almond cake, Lorcan's favorite, a pot of jasmine tea brewing on the stove, and the undeniable fresh scent of blood.

There was no one in the kitchen.

Lorcan rushed around the large table and found the chef lying face down in a pool of blood. There was no sign of his mother.

Tears started to stream down Keeva's face. Her shoulders shook with fear and confusion. "Her wounds . . . yours last night . . ." Her voice broke so badly that Lorcan could hardly make any sense of what she was saying.

"What about me?"

"The wounds on your back last night looked like those." Keeva pointed at the dead body.

"I need you to stay calm for me. Are there other people working in the house?" Lorcan asked, holding Keeva's shoulders.

She nodded.

"But I didn't see anyone on the way to the kitchen."

Keeva blinked in confusion. "But we have Mary in the kitchen, Shaun in the garden, and Susan in . . ."

"Keeva, there is no one else in the house, including Mother. I'm sure of it . . ." Lorcan picked up the handle of the phone mounted on the kitchen's wall. Static. He hung up and turned toward Keeva. "Phone line is dead. Do you have a cell phone?"

She nodded.

"All right, I need you to get the phone, call Father, and then come with me to look for Mother. I can't leave you here by yourself." Keeva nodded and scurried back to her room for the phone. Lorcan trailed right behind her, glancing around and scanning for anything unusual.

Before Keeva had finished dialing Father's number, they heard the bang of a door that had been swung open. They rushed toward the living room. At the door was Lorcan's father. He had a lot more gray hair, making him look wise and formidable, Lorcan noticed. His father had always been a powerful figure in Lorcan's mind. Sometimes too much for his liking.

"I was just about to call you," Keeva said.

"Something happened to your mother." It was a statement, not a question. He approached his father.

"Father," he greeted him, feeling like a robot. He'd never known how to behave in front of his father. He always felt foreign and awkward.

"I can see you're up and well. They took your mother." His father looked at him.

"And how did you know?"

"I'm not a psychic. Someone left a voice mail in my phone. They said they'd taken your mother because you took your girlfriend back home with you."

"I didn't take her. She followed me here because she worried. Someone placed a curse on you and Mother. That's why I had to come back . . ."

"A curse! Jesus Christ, Lorcan, do you hear yourself?"

"Yes, I hear myself clearly. I'm not superstitious, but there are way too many things I can't explain, except by magic. How did you know that I can heal myself, Father?"

"That has nothing to do with magic, you silly lad."

Lorcan stared at his father. Ferris Brody was in his late sixties but possessed the brain of a man in his forties—a mind as sharp as laser. And there wasn't an ounce of sentiment in him.

"You're not worried about Mother?"

"Being out there on your own for that long, you should've gotten wiser, Lorcan. They won't harm your mother until they tell us what they want."

"Isn't it blatantly obvious? They want me to take Orla out of the country again. But there are others who wanted me here. That's why they cursed you and Mother. Are you sure if I take Orla out of here, they'll leave you alone?"

"Do not mention anything about magic in this house ever again, Lorcan. I won't tolerate it. Whoever took your mother won't kill as long as you do what they want."

"I don't know what they want, but they already *have* killed, and there is no guarantee they won't come back." Lorcan raised his voice as his father arched an eyebrow.

"They killed Mary, Father!" Keeva added and pointed toward the kitchen. Ferris's eyes darkened, and he scurried toward the kitchen.

In the kitchen, they found nothing—no dead body and no trace of blood. The teapot had been removed from the hot stove, and the cake had been taken out of the baking tray and put onto a crystal plate. Keeva's body shook. "I saw it . . . we both saw it. Tell him, Lorcan!"

CHAPTER 6

He didn't know what to believe anymore. He used to believe in his own eyes, but what exactly did he see at the riverbank? Who did he kiss? Orla had walked away from him—had that been real or an illusion? And what about his mother? She was still nowhere to be found. Lorcan turned toward his father whose face was hardened as steel. "There was a dead body here, Father, but I don't have any proof."

"I can't say I believe it because there is nothing for me to believe or disbelieve. But they did take your mother, and that's a fact. And if you take your girlfriend out of the country, they might return her."

"Did they tell you that?"

"No."

"You're speculating on Mother's life?"

"What do you want me to think, Lorcan? We told you not to go out with that girl. You took off to find her, and you never came back. Then your mother rambled on all night last night about how she knew you were returning. Then you got here looking like a mess, and the next thing I knew, your mother was gone. I should never have given you to that woman . . ." Ferris ranted and trailed off at the last part as if he hadn't meant to let it slip out.

"*Given* me to her?" he stared at his father.

"I . . ."

Before Ferris could answer, Lorcan gestured for silence. "Please don't answer. I'm happy enough with what I know now." His mind was racing ahead with too many possibilities, none of which he cared for. This was the reality he hadn't wanted to know. "As I said before, someone threatened me with a curse on you and Mother. That's the only reason I came back. If you believe that me taking Orla out of here would solve your problems, then I'll do just that . . . As you wish, Father." His gaze paused on Ferris's face for a brief moment as if gathering some last images into his mind, and then he strode quickly toward the door.

"Lorcan!" Keeva called out and ran to him. She held him tightly just as she had on the day he left so many years ago. She had been a small kid back then, but her squeeze had been just as tight. Lorcan embraced her and kissed her forehead. "You always know how to find me. I'll leave a trail for you."

She nodded and wiped her tears away. Lorcan glanced at his father one last time and exited the house.

***

When Lorcan left the house, he ran back down to the river. It dawned on him now that he had no idea where Orla lived. She had never taken him to her home. They'd always met down by the river, and if what happened at the riverbank yesterday wasn't a hallucination, if it was actually Orla he had seen, then how the hell he was going to find her and take her out of here?

A rustling noise near a clump of bushes caught his attention. He turned around, shivers running down his spine. The noise was coming from behind a blackberry bush, and it made Lorcan freeze. Stepping out in front of him was a large, yellow wolf with red eyes. He didn't know if it was a normal wolf or something magical, but he wasn't going to take any chances.

He backed away a pace or two, as slowly as he could. The wolf advanced and then sat down.

"All right. So you're friendly. But I'm in a very bad mood right now and staring at me isn't helping at all."

The wolf stared at Lorcan for another moment and then spat out something on the ground. It backed up a bit and sat again. Lorcan approached to see what the small object was. He crouched and picked it up. It was unmistakably his mother's wedding ring. He could feel his blood boiling and his body vibrating with rage. The yellow wolf in front of him was obviously some kind of shapeshifter.

"What are you trying to tell me? If you want me to take Orla away, I'm going to do just that."

The wolf growled and bared its teeth.

"You don't want me to do that. What do you want then?"

The wolf stood and turned around.

"You want to take me to my mother?"

It kept walking.

"I'll take that as a yes," Lorcan mumbled and followed the wolf. "I guess I'm going to meet the whole clan of shapeshifters now. I'm assuming you didn't do any harm to my mother. Also, if you decide to shift back into your human form so that you can speak, I have some things to ask you about the woman at the riverbank."

The wolf glanced at Lorcan and then put its head down to the ground again and continued walking.

"I think that woman is a witch—and a bad one." He heard a humming noise of agreement from the wolf. Lorcan chuckled. "I have to admit she was incredibly beautiful. But I would never have kissed her if she hadn't pretended to be Orla . . ."

The wolf growled.

"Yeah, I know. Thanks for the sympathy. I hope Orla understands. It felt as if that woman was raping me . . ."

A low bark came from the animal.

"I'm serious. As soon as I saw she wasn't Orla . . . It doesn't matter how beautiful she was, she was forcing herself . . ."

The wolf came at him like a sudden storm. Lorcan didn't have time to think except to remember he'd lost his gun. He knew fighting the wolf bare-handed wasn't a good idea, so he shifted into his blue fox form. The wolf was in the air and flying toward him, maw gaping. Even though he was only a fox, Lorcan wasn't much smaller than the tawny wolf, and his teeth were just as sharp.

He yelped when the wolf drew first blood, but he reared up on his hind paws and clawed at the wolf's face until it turned its head, then he bit down hard on whatever flesh he could reach. The fight continued for several long minutes, Lorcan trading a wound for every injury he received. Then the wolf made a mistake. He reached to snap at Lorcan's front leg, but when he stepped forward, the large rock he was putting his weight on shifted, causing him to lose his balance and expose his throat to Lorcan. Lorcan didn't hesitate. He moved his head, lightning fast, and caught the wolf by the throat. It went completely limp in his mouth, and he bit down a little harder before he shook the wolf and released his bite.

Lorcan stood still so that the wolf knew he was safe to walk away. He wasn't that generous. But his wounds hurt like hell and he didn't want to fight anymore. Lorcan watched as the wolf limped away, and then he returned to a pile of shredded material that used to be his clothes and lay down in them, nursing his own bite wounds and scratches. He was still amped up from adrenaline, and it felt like he could hear colors and taste sounds. He started to nose around in his shirt to assess the damage it had received. No, these clothes would never be worn again. He sighed.

He would just have to go home as a fox rather than walking in naked. Lorcan picked up the ring in his mouth and trotted home.

***

The house was as quiet as when he had left it. He walked right into the living room in his fox form. His father and his sister were glaring at each other as if they had just finished an argument. They turned and looked at him. Keeva stood there, mouth hanging wide open in shock, apparently unsure whether she should attack this animal or run. His father, on the other hand, sat down in a chair and just looked at him. If Lorcan wasn't mistaken, his father had recognized him right away. There was relief in his father's eyes when he saw Lorcan.

His father wanted him to come back.

Lorcan sat and dropped the ring on the floor.

CHAPTER 7

The haunting sound of an owl ripped through the air and woke Orla. She sat up abruptly and punched at something in front or her. She panted and glanced frantically around. The blurry vision become clear in a short moment. She was sitting in a bed, and the 'thing' she had hit was her distant cousin Alana.

"Oi, you crazy snit!"

Only Alana would call Orla a snit. It made no sense, but it was the nickname she had given Orla when she was just a grumpy kid in black magic class, and she refused to call Orla by any other name.

Orla looked around the room. She didn't recognize the place. "Where am I?"

"Uncle Daly's house."

Her head throbbed in incredible pain. Refraining from a sneer, she asked, "Bradan's father?"

Alana shrugged. "Yes, as long as I've know them, they've been father and son. What's the problem?"

Does Alana seriously not see the problem, or is she just playing dumb? Orla wagered on the latter. If Bradan was going into power in two weeks, having Orla back in the village was the last thing Uncle Daly wanted. Apart from Uncle Daly being a normally calm and collected man, Orla couldn't remember much about him, and she had no way of knowing who was friend and who was foe at the moment. "Where's Maeve?"

"She was the one who messed up your head?"

"What?" Orla straightened up, remembering the black magic that had attacked her in the cemetery. *How did Alana know that?* "What about my head?"

Alana thrust a small mirror toward Orla. "See for yourself. I bet it hurt!"

Orla frowned as she looked at her forehead and saw a nasty wound glaring back at her. It was good that Alana referred to the physical wound, not the black magic. "Did you find me?" Orla asked.

"No. Uncle Daly did. He brought you here and called me. He said he found you at Aunt Siobhan's grave. Only Maeve would lurk around there. That's what I said. But Uncle Daly didn't believe me. He said until he saw it with his own eyes, he wouldn't believe Maeve could do this."

"Do what?"

"Put that dent in your forehead!" Alana waved her arms in the air.

Orla nodded. She saw no reason to explain to Alana that Maeve had just wanted to help her. Between Maeve and Alana, she trusted Maeve more. She rubbed her head. "Do you have a bandage that I can patch this up with?"

Alana clucked her tongue. "You'll need more than that, and I have it ready. Nothing fancy." Alana put both a medical box and a makeup box on the bed. "Bathroom is over there. You'll find clean clothes in there, too. They're mine, but I think we're the same size."

"I don't need makeup. Just need to clean up and sleep for the rest of the night if that's okay."

Alana shook her head. "You have to at least go downstairs and say hi to everyone."

"Everyone?" Orla could feel the hair on the back of her neck stand up.

Alana grinned.

Orla scurried into the bathroom. Staring at her bruised forehead in the mirror, she knew Maeve was right—a storm was brewing her way. She had run off at the age of twelve, leaving her clan in limbo without a rightful leader. *But they had managed to organize and survive,* she told herself now as she had so many times before. She thought people in the clan were better off without a leader. They could live their normal human lives. Why did they have to stay with the clan? The myth was that being with the clan and a new leader appointed at the magical full moon would bring immortality. But she hadn't seen evidence of it yet.

Orla shook her head. Why people would want to live forever in misery was beyond her understanding. But she supposed that living an emotionless life might be a misery to her but a pleasure to others. She couldn't speak for them. She could see the point now after experiencing how much it had hurt to see Lorcan with the other woman. Just the thought of it now made her head start to throb again.

She cleaned up and walked downstairs with Alana. The hallway was too short for her liking. She walked as slowly as she could, but she knew she would get to the living room eventually. A good chunk of her family was here, and they were all staring at her. She could feel the heat of their gazes, and she felt like she had maybe grown an extra head or a tail. But no, she was just an older version of the Orla who had run away at the age of twelve. *What are they staring at?* She wondered.

The laughter and conversation in the room ceased as soon as Orla walked in. The air was as quiet as the calmness experienced before a storm. She could feel it brewing, ready to break on her like crashing waves on rocks. Orla pasted a smiled on her face. "Hi . . ." she said and internally cursed her awkwardness

Uncle Daly approached and gestured toward a chair. "I hope you're feeling better. We won't keep you long. You see, the whole village wants to see you."

An elderly man pushed his way to the front of the crowd and glared at her. "You made a promise when you were younger, and again when you asked for help in London. You will take your place as the head of this family at the next full moon. No more excuses. You will be under watch until this happens because we will not risk you running away again."

"Tony!" Uncle Daly warned in a low voice.

"She was raised for this. We invested so much in her. And she is our best bet," Tony said.

"I am the best bet for what?" Orla asked.

"You don't have a say here," Daly spoke calmly to Tony and ignored Orla's question.

"You just want the post for your son. I knew it," Tony snarled.

"Remember your place, Tony. Regardless, it's Bradan or Orla to lead the clan, you are not in a position to say anything."

"And you are?" Tony glared at him again, but when Daly threw back an even harsher look, Tony turned on his heel and left the room.

No one else said a word. Orla felt the silence pressing down on her like a weight. She could trust

Maeve, but Maeve wasn't allowed to attend the clan meeting. She practised white magic, so within the black magic sorcery clan, Maeve was a 'black sheep'. *How ironic,* Orla thought. Orla realized that without Lorcan, nothing in her life seemed to work in a normal order.

She turned her face away from the family members who still stared at her and tried to give herself a false illusion of some sort of privacy. She wanted the tears to fall without anyone watching, but something told her that that wasn't going to happen. She wanted to run right out the door, but she was sure that would be a bad idea, so she let the thought pass. Orla didn't expect these black magic workers who were supposed to live an emotionless life were going to be gentle with her. But she didn't care for them to gut her alive for a sacrifice, either.

She worked her brain hard to figure out a way out of the situation, but nothing came to mind. "I'm tired. Could I rest for tonight, and then we can resume the conversation tomorrow?"

The room stared at Orla in silence. *Well, it's not an outrageous request!* Orla thought.

"I see no harm in that," said a woman in her late fifties, sitting in the back of the room. If Orla's memory served, that was Aunt Anna, a very distant relative she had hardly talked to when she was a kid. She remembered Anna because she had broken into her conservatory and stolen a few rare plants for an experiment, trying to grow them with milk in her bedroom . Well, the plants had died, and Anna had never figured out where her plants had gone. Orla cleared her throat and tried not to think because if she was not mistaken, the old man sitting near the door was Pete, the shaman of the clan who also could read minds.

Daly looked at Orla. "Okay. We'll talk again tomorrow. Just so you know, I don't have anything against you taking the leadership. The position has always been yours, and it's written in stone. It has been an ordeal to train Bradan and get him up to speed to replace you. But if he can't use the skills in the position, I'm sure he can find use for them elsewhere."

"You don't have to speak for me, Father." Bradan walked into the room.

Orla's jaw dropped. The freckled, red-haired boy had turned into quite a formidable figure.

CHAPTER 8

"Orla," Bradan nodded in greeting. "I'm glad to see you again."

Orla forced a smile and frantically searched her memory for Bradan's talent. *Was he a mind reader? Was he good at chemical compound? Spells?* Nothing came to mind. Orla gave up and forced herself to stop thinking.

"If no one objects, I'll retire to the bedroom," Orla said.

Daly nodded.

"Someone should keep an eye on her," said Anna, her voice was as cold as steel.

"Are you imprisoning me?" Orla raised her voice.

"No, darling, we don't do such things. But it's two weeks to the full moon. I don't want to see the post swinging from one hand to another," Anna said.

"Do you have a preference for the leader, Anna?" Daly cocked an eyebrow in challenge.

"Why would this old woman have a preference for this sort of thing? I just want to be left alone." Anna stood.

Braden wrapped his arm around Orla's waist protectively. "I think we should let Orla rest. I'll take her upstairs."

Anna chuckled. "You speak like a leader already."

Bradan stared at her. "I'm prepared for whatever comes my way, Aunty."

Anna gave Bradan a dismissive look. "I think you should let Alana stay with Orla tonight. I want to be sure you won't strangle her in her sleep."

"Don't accuse my son of something like that!" Daly raised his voice and advanced on Anna. Bradan stopped his father.

"All right. I think it's a good idea that Alana stay tonight . . . Alana?" Bradan asked.

Everyone turned to look at Alana, who was examining her manicure and looked as if she would rather be anywhere else.

"Alana!" Braden called again.

"Huh?" Alana jumped.

"Would you mind staying here tonight with Orla?"

"What? Why?"

"We just need you to stay with her . . . to make sure she's okay."

Alana rolled her eyes, then forced a smile and said, "Of course. I'm sure it's going to be a pleasant night." Then she turned on her heel and marched up the stairs. Bradan shook his head.

"Come on." He reached his hand out to Orla. She grabbed it and followed him up the stairs.

Braden entered the bedroom first, glancing around. "I've already been in here. The room is fine, Bradan," Orla said.

He shrugged. "You never know. The clan has developed a lot since you've been away, and there are a lot of people in our clan who I don't care for."

Orla nodded. Bradan was so mature now. Remembering when she and other girls picked on him when they were kids, she smiled on the inside.

"You should go to bed." His voice was deep and enticing. Orla shook the uncomfortable thought off and headed for the bed.

Bradan opened the window and looked around. Seemingly satisfied with what he saw, he closed the door, locked it, and exited the room.

Alana had already lay down on the inside wall of the bed, and she'd put a long pillow in the middle, suggesting that Orla could take the outside half. Alana quickly dozed off.

Orla stayed awake for a long time, listening to Alana's even breathing. When she was sure her bed mate was really asleep, she hopped off the bed and moved to the window. The roof arched over a porch below. Orla stepped out onto the roof and inched toward the edge. She looked down and let out a sigh of relief. It wasn't too high up from the ground. She looked up to the clear Irish sky in the middle of the night, breathed in the clear air, and bent down to make a jump to the ground below.

Damn it! Orla cursed in her head as she hit the ground.

On the porch, next to the door, Bradan was sitting on a chair, smoking.

She hadn't surprised him in the least by both trying to flee the clan in the middle of the night and landing from the sky in front of him. He squashed out his cigarette and smiled. Orla smiled back.

"You took longer than I thought you would," Bradan said.

Orla had her hands on her hips. "So you're a mind reader. Handy!"

He chuckled. "I wish I had such talent. My father trained me well in logical deduction. I don't have any magical talent. You'd be a much better leader than me because you're a natural."

"But I don't want to do it. Everyone knows that. You don't sound like you want to do it, either."

Bradan merely smiled.

"Oh . . . you *do* want the post!" Orla said. "That's good. Can we swap? Can you just tell them?" Orla put on the most gracious smile she could.

"I can't, Orla. If you want to see your man, I'll take you to him."

"Why help me?"

"You said it yourself—I want the post, and you don't. If you leave again, then the post will be mine. Simple!" Bradan smiled.

Orla narrowed her eyes. "I can go by myself. All you have to do is to pretend you didn't see me."

Bradan shook his head. "I can't let you go through that wedge of the woods by yourself. There's a nasty group of shapeshifters lurking around there lately."

Orla hesitated, and Bradan continued. "Now, I might kill you in the woods in order to take the position, but between me and these shapeshifters, I'm a much safer bet. If you want to escape, now is a better time. Tomorrow, more family members will come. It will become more difficult."

"Why are you helping me, really?"

"As I said, I want the post, so I have to help you escape." Bradan grinned. Now Orla wished she were a mind reader. It would certainly be a handy set of skills to have. Bradan appeared to be good, but he could be dangerous. She was sure her magic was better than his, because she had been trained earlier. Plus she had some white magic tricks she had gotten from Maeve.

He was right, however. The shapeshifters in the woods were dangerous. She guessed they were related to Bricius. Bricius had cursed Lorcan's parents. His clan here must have something to do with it. The more she thought about it, the more the option Bradan offered appeared to be more attractive. Orla put her doubts aside and nodded.

CHAPTER 9

Lorcan opened his eyes and sprung off the bed. He had gotten back to his room and crashed in order to heal his wounds from the fight with the yellow wolf. He couldn't have been out for long, he thought. There were so many questions he wanted to ask his father and his sister, and he was sure they had some for him, too. There was no way to have a conversation when he was in his fox form.

Roy had told him once that most werefoxes didn't remember much of what happened when they were in the animal form, but some did. Mori had perfect memories and was well aware of what she was doing in any form because she was an alpha. Roy had such memory, too, but he was half fox and half wolf. Lorcan knew he was in none of those scenarios. As Roy had told him, he was different. In his fox form, his brain functioned normally and with clarity.

He put on the clothes he used to wear during his teenage years, grateful he had built himself up in the right places. His T-shirt fit more like a muscle shirt now, and his baggy jeans now fit him perfectly.

"Lorcan!" Keeva screamed out his name from the living room, a terrible sound that tore his heart and got him to his feet, running downstairs. Next to the fireplace, his father sat on the reading chair, holding his mother's wedding ring in one hand and a pistol on the other hand. His eyes were bloodshot, a sure sign of that he was trying to hang on to the last thread of consciousness. He didn't know where he'd seen this before, but he knew he had seen it.

Something was eating at his father's mind, and he was trying to fight it.

"She's dead. They've killed her." Ferris grunted out the words and pointed the gun to his temple. "It's my fault." Tears welled up in his eyes.

"Father, please don't do that. Give me the gun," Keeva cried.

Lorcan approached his father slowly. "Father, Mother is not dead. Someone tried to help us. That's why they gave us her wedding ring. Please calm down and give me the gun. We need to talk."

"It's my fault." Ferris brandished the gun. "I shouldn't have given you to her."

"What do you mean by that, Father?" Lorcan inched closer.

"Don't come near me. I knew I shouldn't have signed up for that. When I gave you to your mother, she was so happy, but I should have known that it wouldn't last long. You're such a disaster." He pointed the gun at Lorcan.

Keeva hissed and pulled at Lorcan, but he shoved her behind his back. "You adopted me?"

Ferris laughed. "I wish it's that simple... There is only one way to end this." He pointed the gun to his head.

"No!" Lorcan flew at his father and tackled him. He knocked Ferris to the floor and took the gun off of his father. From the floor, his father looked up at Lorcan with eyes that weren't his.

"Remember the curse?" The voice croaking out of Ferris was familiar. It was Bricius's voice. "No one can break my curse. Someone will die. I curse . . ."

"Stop." Lorcan yelled and muffled his father's mouth with his hand. His father wriggled hard. Keeva heard what her father just said, she jumped in helping Lorcan. Ferris roared, kicked and moved with incredible strength, the strength Lorcan knew wasn't his father's. He didn't know how long he and Keeva could hang on to this.

Then he felt a wedge of cold breeze coming from the door. A woman appeared from nowhere stormed right into the living room uninvited.

"That's black magic. You can't fight that using physical strength," the woman said.

"I don't do magic. Who the hell are you?" Lorcan asked.

"I'm Maeve, Orla's cousin. I'm here to let you know someone is using mind-control and black magic on Orla, making her hate you and curse you. That same magic is working its dark energy on that man."

"You sound like you know what you are talking about. Can you help my father?" Lorcan asked.

Ferris grew stronger and almost pushed Lorcan and Keeva back.

"That's black magic. I don't know how to break it. If Orla keeps thinking about you, she's going to burst into flames."

Ferris growled and pushed and Lorcan and Keeva.

"You have to help my father first before I can do anything else," Lorcan said.

"You have to knock him out. That way you can temporarily keep him under control."

"You want me to hit my father?"

"The thing in his head is not your father."

"I don't give a shit, I won't hit my father." Lorcan shoved hard and pushed Ferris into a chair. "Get something to tie him," he asked Keeva. Lorcan all but sat on Ferris to hold him down. He still had a hand on his mouth to stop him from chanting a curse. Keeva came back with rope and tapes from the tool shed. They tied him up and stuffed his mouth with cloths.

Maeve stood there with hands on hips. "And how long do you think you can keep him like that?"

"I'll find Orla, and we'll work out a way to handle this."

"You don't sound like you totally dismiss the possibility of using magic."

"I don't have a choice," Lorcan growled. "Can you take me to Orla?"

"I can, but it's not going to help the situation. Before I figure out how to control the curse, you guys are best not seeing each other."

"If Orla couldn't figure it out, how can you ?"

Maeve smiled. "Are you saying I'm not as good as she is?"

"I don't know you. I just want to be realistic. They must want her to lead the clan for good reasons. There must be something she does that's better than others."

Maeve laughed. "I can see how she's falling head over heels for you. You guys are made for each other."

Lorcan narrowed his eyes. "I don't believe she's kept in touch with her family over the years. You seem to know too much about us."

Maeve shook her head. "We can communicate via a psychic channel. You wouldn't understand."

"Can you use white magic to help my father?"

"I'm not sure if I'm strong enough to go against them. That's why I'm here to tell you to stay away from Orla. I need a bit of time to figure things out, and the two-week deadline is coming faster than I care for."

"That two-week event again. What the hell is that?"

"It's the full moon when the clan chooses a leader. The other candidate is okay, but he's not as good as Orla. I don't think he's over-ambitious and would harm Orla or you to protect the leadership post, though"

"*He?*" Lorcan asked.

"Yes, as far as I know, Bradan is a male." Maeve raised an eyebrow. "I read in Orla's mind before she passed out about her encounter with you and another woman . . ."

Maeve's voice started to echo. Feeling the cold air creeping up his back, Lorcan withdrew and mentally braced himself to fight what was to come. His vision wavered slightly, and his head start to go numb. *You can't use the same trick twice on me!* He looked at Maeve, and a surge of lust rose inside him. *Control!* Lorcan distanced himself. The second he let the feeling grow because he thought the woman at the riverbank had been Orla was the very second he lost control of his body and mind.

CHAPTER 10

Lorcan shook his head, trying to stay alert. He felt as if he was drowning in deep water. He turned toward Maeve. Her image flickered. And then in front of him was Orla. She smiled, and he couldn't breathe. His head was going to explode. He swayed. Orla approached to help him. But he knew it wasn't Orla. He stepped back.

"Stay away from me."

The image of the woman flickered and returned as Maeve.

"Lorcan!"

He heard Orla's voice from the door. Lorcan looked up and saw Orla with a man. This might not be her, he thought. "Stay away from me," he repeated.

Orla approached.

"Stay right there!" he yelled and that stopped Orla in her tracks. *That's how she looks when she's surprised. That's the real Orla.* "Orla," he whispered just before the hot rage took over. He hadn't experienced this before. He staggered back. The urge to kill and destroy consumed him. He hated as if he had never hated before. *Why is Orla with this man? Who is he? Is he using the black magic on her and on his father?*

"You did this to my father!" Lorcan roared.

"I did what?" the man asked.

Lorcan staggered back, leaning against the wall, breathing heavily. He had to force his mind out of his body. He could see himself now—he looked like a madman, bloodshot eyes, yelling profanity, rushing at Orla, Maeve, and the man who had just walked into the house with Orla. He could see himself out of control, but he couldn't stop it. He saw a tear roll down Orla's face.

He had made her cry. Again.

Then he lost concentration for a second. That was all it took. He was sucked back into his body, and the next thing he knew, he had shot two waves of electric current at the strange man. To Lorcan's surprise, the man was as calm as still water. He waved his hand, and it seemed as if the current had hit a metal shield and diverted. It didn't come back at him but headed in his father's direction.

The heat burned the rope and set his father free. Charged with rage, his father grabbed the gun lying on the table and aimed it at Keeva.

That was all Lorcan could see.

At that very moment, his mind was as clear as crystal. He could shoot the electric wave and burn his father into ashes to stop him from pulling the trigger on Keeva. There was no other option except . . .

As quick as lightning, Lorcan grabbed at Keeva, pulling her backward. The momentum pushed him forward and into the path of the bullet. He could see the scene in slow motion. The penetration of the bullet into his chest wasn't bad at all. It was like a prick of pain at the entry point, and then the pressure of something disintegrating into his body, and then the heat of his own blood.

He slumped to his knees. Lorcan had a feeling he wouldn't be able to heal himself from this injury very quickly . . . if at all.

His mind was perfectly clear. It seemed as if the magic—or whatever it was that had caused the craziness in the room—had vanished. Everything was back to normal.

He fell backward and into Keeva's arms. His father appeared to snap back to reality as if the demon had just left him. And Orla, he could see her approaching him with tears on her face and determined eyes.

Lorcan leaned into Keeva's arms. Orla crouched in front of him and held his hands. "It's not too bad. You just need to crash and you'll heal," she said with a shaky voice.

"I don't want you anymore. I don't want to see you anymore. Leave me, Orla," he said.

"No way in hell I'll leave you. That trick doesn't work on me, Lorcan."

He didn't have enough energy to pull his hands from Orla's.

"Maeve!" Lorcan called out.

"Yes. You broke the black magic, Lorcan. If there was a black magic curse on your father, you broke it."

"Great news!" He smiled weakly. "Can I break the curse on Orla?"

Maeve said nothing.

Lorcan nodded. "All right. If I can't fix this, I don't want Orla near me. Can you keep her away, please?"

Maeve nodded.

"Maeve!" Orla hissed and withdrew when she saw Maeve glance at Bradan. Bradan approached from behind and snatched Orla off the ground. While Orla kicked, screamed, and struggled, trying to get out of Bradan's grip, Lorcan nodded a thank you to Bradan. In a short moment, Maeve and Bradan dragged Orla out of the house.

"Keeva!" Lorcan called his sister.

"Yes?"

"I don't want anyone to use magic on me. Promise me you'll keep those people away from me—even if I die because of it."

"I promise." Keeva's voice cracked with tears.

"I don't want a doctor, either"

"If you don't take magic, you have to go to the hospital," Keeva cried.

His father crouched in front of him. "Lorcan, tell me what you need." His eyes were calm and still, but his hands trembled.

Lorcan gazed into his father's eyes. "Am I your real son?"

"Yes. I can't take back the bullet, but I would like to take back what I said. You are my son, and I love you. Now if you want to know where you came from and your special conditions, you have to stay alive."

Lorcan smiled. His father was the same, a man with a mind as hard as steel. The world was blurring by the second. His father's image flickered in front of him.

"I'll have to take you to the hospital," Keeva said.

"No. I can't go to the hospital. I need Riley."

"Who?" his father asked.

"Your friend in London?" Keeva asked.

He wanted to answer his sister's question but darkness claimed him.

CHAPTER 11

Keeva checked Lorcan's bullet wound one last time and pulled the blanket up to cover him. Unlike the wounds on his back, this bullet wound was still bleeding and didn't appear to be healing. She didn't need medical knowledge to guess that regardless of whatever special ability her brother had, the wound wouldn't heal with the bullet still inside it. That was why Lorcan wanted Riley. From the little information she had, her brother's best friend Riley was a medical doctor.

Was he her blood brother after all? Where had he come from?

Things had happened so quickly she didn't have time to ask her father. He had gone into town to meet with someone who could help find Mother and send people to London for Riley. He had a lot of connections, and she hadn't yet seen anything her father couldn't handle. Well, maybe only the earlier incident.

Father didn't believe in anything magical. But Mother was a believer of magic, although she had never admitted it.

She needed to find Riley now, but she couldn't leave Lorcan here by himself, unconscious. She could go to the internet, but looking for what? There was something that looked like a watch that Lorcan always had with him. He had so many technological gadgets; she couldn't keep up with him. She stared at Lorcan's wrist unit, and it stared back at her. Then the screen flashed with an incoming message alert. She touched a green button. The screen flashed in red, punctuated by a loud beep. "Unauthorized access." The message startled her so much that she almost threw the device on the floor. She tucked it underneath Lorcan's pillow.

"Unauthorized my butt," she mumbled. Could she cut the bullet out herself? Keeva dismissed the thought. One minor surgery on an injured wild dog's leg when she was a little kid didn't warrant experience to cut her brother's chest open. She wiped the sweat on Lorcan's forehead and saw that his temperature had increased considerably. It was obvious that his body was trying its best to heal itself, but it couldn't do so with a foreign object inside his chest.

Keeva was in desperate need to hit something now, or maybe just to yell. Then she heard the doorbell. She cursed. People working in the house had mysteriously disappeared since yesterday, and their phone line in the house had been cut off. This may be a routine delivery guy who couldn't get into the kitchen from the back door.

Keeva opened the door. In front of her was not the delivery man but a man in his thirties and a boy of about nine or ten.

"Hello, my name is Riley."

"Riley? My brother's friend?"

"You must be Keeva."

The boy's eyes welled up with tears, and before Keeva could ask anything, he ran past her into the house. "I need to see Uncle Lorcan," his voice echoed back after he vanished up the stairs.

"Hey!" Keeva yelled. Riley grabbed her elbow, and when Keeva stopped and turned to look at him, he released her arm.

"I'm sorry. Lorcan was shot, wasn't he? I can help."

Keeva couldn't stop the tears filling her eyes. She wasn't sure if it was because of the anxiety or the fear. But the world around her had been moving too fast, she had lost her bearings.

Without a response from her, Riley pressed on. "My son, Noah, he had a vision . . . he saw Lorcan get shot, and he's been nagging me for three days to come here. I know you probably won't believe me, but . . ."

"I believe you."

"Oh . . ."

"Yes, I said I believe you. I've seen some strange things here my whole life. A psychic vision doesn't surprise me. Please help Lorcan. The bullet is in his chest, but he didn't want any medical doctor except you."

Riley nodded and shifted the heavy bag he was carrying. "Is he upstairs?" Riley asked while heading toward the stairs.

Keeva rushed ahead to lead. "How did Noah know where to go?"

"As much as I hate admitting it, he's a psychic. I'm not." The bag he was carrying was so heavy he almost lost his balance on the stairs.

Riley chuckled. "Sorry, I didn't know what I'd need, so there's a portable hospital in my bag."

***

Keeva and Riley found Noah in front of Lorcan's room, tears staining his face. Keeva crouched down to his level. "Lorcan told me if I could get your father here, he'll be okay."

Noah nodded. He stepped aside to allow Riley entrance to the room. Keeva followed and felt a tug at her hand. It was Noah. His little hand was cold, damp, and a little shaky. She wrapped her hand around his and rubbed it to keep him warm. Noah looked up at her. His light green eyes were so much like his father's. Innocence. That was all Keeva could see. But what surprised her the most was that his hand in hers felt so natural.

Riley turned around, looking at Keeva after examining the wound.

"Oh God, please don't tell me you can't do it," Keeva said.

"The wound is so close to his heart. I'm afraid I have to do this at a hospital. It's too risky here."

"He doesn't want to go to a hospital."

"He always says that . . ."

On the bed, Lorcan stirred and opened his eyes. "Riley . . . I knew you'd come . . ." His voice was barely audible.

"Lorcan, I have to take you to the hospital. This is a major surgery—I can't do it here."

"Just take the bullet out. If I survive that, I'll heal quickly . . ."

"But I don't think you can survive it."

"I've had worse. Trust me. Just take the bullet out."

"I've seen his wounds heal themselves, Riley," Keeva added.

Riley shook his head.

"Please," Lorcan said and passed out again.

"Please do what he said, Dad!" Noah cried.

"Did you have another vision, Noah?" Riley asked.

Noah shook his head.

"Yesterday he came home with nasty wounds on his back. But in a couple of hours, they healed as if they'd never been there. But he can't do it with a bullet in his chest, Riley," Keeva said.

"Are you sure?"

Keeva nodded.

"Okay. Please give me some space and wait outside."

Keeva picked Noah up, left of the room, and closed the door behind her.

CHAPTER 12

"Please keep an eye on her. I mean it, Alana." Bradan put an unconscious Orla on the bed.

Alana stood up from a comfortable reading chair in the corner of the room. "What happened to her?"

"Maeve knocked her out."

"Again? I knew it. Violent bitch."

"She was only trying to help."

Alana's hands were on her hips. "She's a white witch, Bradan!"

"She tried to help, and what she did was very complicated. Not just watching Orla as you do."

81

"You helped her run away. You talked to Maeve and let her do this to Orla. Now you're blaming me for not watching her!"

"I'm not blaming you for anything. If I could watch, I'd do so myself."

"I want to go home. I have a life, Bradan." Alana strode toward the door.

"Please!"

"What about all the aunts in the family?"

"You're the only young one, Alana. I can't put an aunt in here with Orla."

Alana rolled her eyes and walked around the room in agitation. "So what am I supposed to do when she wants to leave? Knock her on her ass?"

Bradan shrugged. "Apparently we can't just lock the door because she got off the roof last time. We might have to tie her up."

"You've got to be kidding me!"

"Do you have any suggestions?"

Alana rolled her eyes again. "What if she puts a spell on me and makes me free her? Or worse, what if she curses me?"

"Damn it, Alana, you're a sorceress. Don't you practice at all?"

Alana couldn't find a word to say back at Bradan. She stomped toward the desk and grabbed her books and her bag. "Well, if I'm not mistaken, you're asking for my help. I'm not good at black magic and will never be. I don't care for it. This clan's business is none of mine. Now get out of my hair!" She stormed toward the door.

Bradan barred her way. "Oh, come on. I'm sorry, Alana. Just stay one more day, and I'll see what I can do."

Alana glared at him.

"Please!"

"Never look down at me again!"

"Never. I promise."

"You owe me."

"Definitely."

"I need my laptop."

"What?"

"Do you seriously want me to sit here for two weeks, melting in boredom?"

"Okay. I'll get it for you."

Alana grinned. Bradan shook his head and left the room.

***

The sound of a computer game woke Orla. She opened her eyes to find that her hands were tied to the bar of a headboard. In the corner of the room, Alana was glued to her laptop. Orla sat up on the bed, but that didn't break Alana's concentration on her game.

It was rare that Orla had a chance to observe her distant cousin. She'd make a perfect movie star, Orla thought. Long sandy hair, big blue eyes, oval face, and perfect lips. She could play a princess in one of the Disney fairy tales. Orla cleared her throat, and that caught Alana's attention. She turned the volume of the game down.

"Damn, one more level, and I'll beat this bastard," she mumbled.

"Go ahead. I can wait." Orla jiggled at the chains on her wrists.

Alana shook her head. "That's all right. I can always come back and beat the hell out of him later." She grinned.

"What game?"

"You know games?"

Orla chuckled. "Not really. But Lorcan is a game fanatic."

Alana's eyes sparked with curiosity. "Really? You should introduce us. When you become the leader, you won't be able to be with him anymore. I can take him. A good gamer is hard to come by."

"I'll consider it." Orla smiled.

"Please do. Are you hungry?"

Orla shook her head while Alana yawned.

"Bradan told me you went to Oxford. Why come back if you don't care about the clan's politics?" Orla asked.

Alana chuckled. "I miss that world. Really. My parents died. I'm sure Bradan told you that, too. I came back to make arrangements for the funeral. I thought it would be a short trip. Then one thing led to another. No one was taking care of the business they left behind. Before I know it, I was stuck here."

"Don't you want to go back?"

"Of course. Soon, actually. I promised to help out with the ceremony and then, after that, I'll be back to London. I've sold the family business here. Two more weeks, and I'm out of here." Alana grinned.

Orla smiled. "I can sense there's a man involved."

Alana blushed. "Can't tell you."

"I'm jealous, Alana. I don't want to take the post. Why can't they let Bradan? He wants it."

Alana shrugged. "It's not for me to say."

Orla adjusted her position. "I need to go to the bathroom."

"Don't try anything, Snit."

"You want me to pee right here?"

Orla smiled because she could feel Alana had put up her protective spell so she couldn't manipulate her mind. She opened the chain. "Try anything, and I'll hurt you, Orla."

Orla went to the bathroom and closed the door.

Inside, she turned on the tap and looked in the mirror to examine the bruise on her forehead. She waited for a bit and then cast her spell, a white spell she'd learned from Maeve. Shortly, she heard a thunk on the floor. She turned the water off and rushed out.

Alana had fallen on her face on the floor. Orla checked to see if she had hit her head on anything. Seeing no damage apart from a small bruise on Alana's forehead, Orla pulled the blanket off the bed and tucked Alana in. Then she crawled out onto the roof again. This time, she dipped her head down low and checked to ensure Bradan wasn't around.

Then she hopped down to the ground and darted into the night.

CHAPTER 13

Keeva sat in a reading chair in a smaller room upstairs. She couldn't do much until she heard the news from Riley. It had been a while. She should feed Noah. She looked down and saw that Noah had fallen asleep while curling against her side. The kid had just met her, but the strange thing was that it didn't feel unusual at all that he displayed such affection in his interaction with her. Keeva always did well with animals, but she didn't think she would do well with kids. *What happened to your*

mom? she thought as she looked at Noah's thick lashes, freckled cheeks, and fair skin. *She must be beautiful.* She played with Noah's hair but stopped when he stirred.

As soon as Riley walked into the reception room, Keeva sprung to her feet. Riley's hair spiked up as he raked his hands through it, and there was a blood smear on his face. "How is he?" Keeva asked.

Riley breathed out heavily. "Alive when I left. I took the bullet out, but I'm not sure about this at all. He lost a lot of blood."

Keeva darted toward Lorcan's room. Riley trailed behind. "I sedated him," he said, "so he'll be out for a while. But the most important thing is that the bleeding has stopped . . ." He trailed off when he got into the room and saw that the incision on Lorcan's chest that he had just stitched up had already begun to form scar tissue. The wound was healing by the second—right in front of Riley's eyes. "What the f—" Riley began but stopped himself when he saw Noah approach the bed, looking at Lorcan.

Keeva turned around. "Thank you." She tiptoed over and hugged Riley.

"You're welcome," he mumbled awkwardly when she released him.

She cleared her throat and pointed at his face. "You've got some blood . . ."

"Oh." Riley wiped randomly and missed the mark.

"Let me." Keeva pulled out her handkerchief and wiped mark away. She bit the inside of her mouth and looked away after she finished. The contact was too close for her comfort. She cleared her throat again. "Lorcan's wound will heal quite quickly as you can see. But it would be—"

"I'll stay until he's up and about," Riley interrupted.

"Oh . . . thanks. I'll show you to your room."

"Yes, please." Riley smiled.

He had a killer smile, Keeva thought, cursing silently. "This way, please." She pointed toward the door and scurried out.

***

Later, Keeva turned on the kitchen light and braced herself against the door frame on the off chance she'd see another dead body on the floor.

But there was no dead body on the floor this time. She exhaled a sigh of relief and searched the cabinet for something with which she could cook a meal. It dawned on her at that point that the delivery man hadn't come, but it wasn't a big deal because the chef always kept enough stock available to make a feast.

Keeva frowned at the cabinet. Unlike her mother, cooking wasn't a skill she could earn a living with. She survived on what she cooked when she was in college because she didn't really have a choice. Hearing a noise at the door, Keeva turned around to see Noah standing there wearing his backpack.

"Where are you going?"

"I need some food."

Keeva uttered another internal curse. She had known it would come to this. How could she explain to the guests that she had found the chef dead in the kitchen, and therefore none of the house staff had come to work today? "Well, sure. Come in. Sit down." She pointed to the kitchen table.

"The food isn't for me." Noah placed his bag on a chair and pulled out the most beautiful kitten she had ever seen. He put the kitten on the table. "We were in a hurry, and I forgot to pack his food. He eats what we eat, but he doesn't like milk at all."

Keeva sat down next to him. The cat looked her up and down, seemingly judging whether she could be trusted. "I can take care of him." If her cooking was bad, at least the cat couldn't complain. "What's his name?"

"Aris. Short for Aristotle."

"You named the kitten after a Greek philosopher?"

"Yes. Aris is a very deep thinker. He just doesn't tell you what he's thinking."

"How do you know that?"

"Well, if he doesn't like something, he'll find a way to let you know."

"Humm . . ." Now she started to worry about the food she was going to feed this little kitten. She would go with the safest bet—a sandwich. The kind that required no cooking.

"Would you like a sandwich?" she asked.

"Do you have ham, cheese, and tomato?"

"Sure, I do."

"Toasted, please?"

"You're too demanding, Noah." Riley stood at the door, giving his son a disapproving look.

"It's easy enough," said Keeva. "But I can't guarantee anything fancier than that!" She stood up to make the sandwich. "And what would you like, Riley?"

"Anything is good. I'm easy."

She smiled. "Why don't I make you my favorite?"

"Thank you. I'm sure I'll love it." Riley smiled and scratched Aris behind his ears. Aris purred so loud it made everyone laugh.

"Come on, you seriously don't even care what I'm going to feed you?" Keeva asked.

Riley shook his head. "I do care about what I put in my body. It's an occupational quirk. But it's merely the nutrition I think about and not so much tastes or preference."

Keeva scowled. "I feel sorry for you, Riley. Even Aris here has preferences."

Riley laughed. "Yes. That cat has preferences in *everything*. You should have seen his reaction when I called him Edward."

"Really?" Keeva looked at Aris, and she swore she saw the cat scowling at Riley. He saw it, too, and laughed. *He has such hearty laughs*, Keeva thought. Honest and from the belly, a giving-it-all kind of laugh. She shook her head, trying to clear out the inappropriate thoughts that threatened to invade her mind. "Well, given you won't tell me what you like, you're going to be stuck with my favorite—a tuna and cucumber sandwich."

Riley's laughter stopped instantly, and the smile vanished from his face.

"Not good?" she asked.

"Oh no . . . I mean yes, I'd like the sandwich." Riley said nothing else. He grabbed Aris, put him on his lap, and stroked his back. But Aris was no longer purring.

Suddenly the sense of death engulfed her. The room started to spin, and she couldn't breathe. She could sense death occasionally, but it had never been this strong. The plate she was holding slipped out of her hand and shattered on the floor. She stormed out the kitchen door to the back garden.

The cool air made her feel a bit better, but she was still quite dazed. In a corner of the garden stood a beautiful woman. She looked at Keeva with a smile on her face.

"Who are you?" she asked.

"I'm Michelle."

"I don't know you."

"You do. Not now . . . but in the future, you'll know me."

"What are you talking about?"

"You *are* me. Take care of Riley and Noah." The woman turned around and vanished into thin air. Then the world turned completely black. She couldn't feel anything except the sensation of floating in the nothingness.

CHAPTER 14

Sounds gradually came back to Keeva, and along with it, the familiar sense of air and life. She opened her eyes and found herself in Riley's arms. He was carrying her. She shifted in his arms. "Put me down. I'm fine."

"No, you're not. You fainted in the kitchen."

He was using what people often called his doctor's tone, and the best way to handle it was to be obedient. Keeva said nothing. Riley lay her down on the sofa and directed, "Stay down." He stopped her when she tried to sit up. "You cut your hand on

the broken plate. I'll get something to patch it up."
Keeva noted that her left arm was bleeding. As Riley
left, he signaled Noah and pointed at her. Noah
nodded and came to sit on the coffee table beside
Keeva.

"He always liked that?"

Noah rolled his eyes and nodded. "My friends at
school used to call him Mr. Serious. But he just
cares. Too much sometimes."

"You let your friends call your dad that?"

Noah shrugged. "They stopped after a while."

Aris approached, hopped on the coffee table, sat
next to Noah, and started washing himself. Keeva
narrowed her eyes. "I know how kids act. Your
friends wouldn't just stop calling your dad names
because you asked them to. What did you do to
convince them?"

"Nothing. Maybe some weird things showed up
in their lunchboxes. That happens to naughty boys,
you know."

Keeva laughed.

"You saw my mom, didn't you?" Noah's tone was
exactly the same as when he had told her about his
friends' lunchboxes. The psychic kid must have
lived with weird things his whole life. It had become

a part of him. Keeva sat up and looked into his eyes. He looked straight back at her, waiting for an answer.

"How does your father handle your visions?"

"I'd never told him before. But they started to cause migraines, and it got so severe that Dad thought I had a brain tumor. So I told him about my visions. He believed me. Since then, the migraines have stopped . . . Are tuna and cucumber sandwiches really your favorite?"

"Yes."

Noah nodded. "It's my mom's favorite, too. Dad doesn't like them, but he pretended to in order to please Mom."

She smiled. "That's very sweet. They must have been very happy together."

Noah nodded. "Before I was born, they were so happy. Mom told me everything. What they did. Where they went. She said Dad was broken when she left him, and if I'm a good boy, I'll take care of him."

"I'm sure you're a good boy. See, you stayed here and watched me just like he asked you to. You must miss your mom very much. When did she pass away?" She tucked a strand of curly hair back behind Noah's ear.

"When she gave birth to me. That's what Dad said."

"So . . . you talked to her . . . spirit?"

Noah nodded and a tear rolled down his face. "But she's stopped seeing me for months. I don't know why. I must have done something wrong." More tears rolled down his face.

"No, no, sweetie. I know she has her reasons." She reached out, pulled Noah into her lap, and cuddled him while he sobbed. It hadn't been for just a short period of time that he hadn't seen his mother, it had been a long while. He had lived with the vision of a dead woman for his entire life. She rocked the boy on her lap, rubbing his back to soothe him and thinking about her own mother.

Riley came back and stared at the scene before him. When Keeva stopped rubbing, Noah turned around and saw his father. He stood up, wiped his tears. Riley crouched. "What happened, Noah?"

"Nothing. I'd like to go to bed now." Noah walked out of the room. Aris trailed right behind him.

"I'll be right with you," Riley said.

"Don't need you," Noah's voice echoed down from the stairs.

Riley turned and looked at Keeva. "What did he just say?"

Keeva said nothing. He'd heard the boy well enough. Riley sat on the sofa and reached out his hand. "Let me see. I'll patch it up."

She snatched the medical kit from his hand. "I can do it myself, thanks. You go after Noah."

"No, it was just a tantrum. He'll get over it. He has to grow up sooner or later."

"He misses his mother. He's lonely. It's more than a tantrum, Riley."

Riley stood up. "You know nothing about us, Keeva."

"I know enough to know that you let your son starve emotionally because your heart was broken when your wife died."

His eyes darkened, and his face hardened. "I'm doing my best to give him whatever he wants. But I'm not his mother, and there's nothing I can do about it."

"Yes, there *are* things you can do to fix it."

Riley gave her a dismissive look and turned on his heel.

"Hey!" she called out loud enough to stop him in his tracks.

"What?" he growled back.

"You might think I know nothing about the pain of losing someone, that Lorcan and I come from privilege and have never had a hard day in our lives."

"I love Lorcan like my brother, but which part of what you said isn't true?" his voice was cold as steel.

"My mother has been missing for two days. Father went crazy and shot Lorcan. And now he's gone into town to look for Mother and hasn't answered my calls for hours. There was a dead body in the kitchen one minute, and then it had disappeared the next. I couldn't even call the cops because they would think I'm crazy. I can't look for my mother because I have no idea where to look."

"I'm so sorry."

"Your pain was so enormous that you saw nothing else. My mother's been missing for only two days, and it hurts so much. Imagine your son living with that his whole life."

"I . . ."

"No, don't say anything to me. I'm not in the mood to discuss who can handle more pain." She

101

stomped out of the room. She didn't look back, but she knew he stood there for a while, staring after her.

CHAPTER 15

Orla ran as fast as she could in the woods. She remembered the general direction of Lorcan's house. If her calculations were right, she would be there in no time. The image of the bullet hitting him replayed countless times in her head and burned like fuel that made her run even faster. She knew he had to survive first in order for the wound to heal. When they were on the island and he was shot by arrows, Ciaran had to pull them out so that his wound could start healing. *Who would do it for him this time?* Removing a bullet wasn't exactly the kind of skill that just anyone had.

Suddenly, she smelled smoke. Someone was nearby. She caught a glimpse of a fire and crept among the trees to get closer. She recognized Uncle Daly and Bradan. They appeared to be arguing, but she was too far away to hear anything. Uncle Daly paced back and forth, arms waving in the air. Bradan appeared to be listening and then responding, but he didn't seem to agree on whatever it was they were arguing about.

When Orla was about to move on with her task at hand, she saw a large shadow leap at Uncle Daly from behind. It was too dark for her to tell what it was, but she could tell from the shadow that the animal was enormous. Bradan physically attacked the animal.

Why didn't he use his magic? He ought to have some skills!

Orla darted in their direction with caution. She had nothing on her that resembled a respectable weapon, but she could throw fireballs, which by all means would be more effective than clawing back at the wild animal as Bradan was doing. When she was close enough, she threw her first ball at the backside of the creature.

It roared and turned, looking at her.

She could see it now. It was an enormous eagle with reptilian skin. "You're goddamn ugly!" Orla said and threw another fireball. The creature flapped its wings and lifted itself off the ground. Before it released Daly, its claw ripped his body apart. Bradan screamed in fury and charged at the creature. It swung a wing and threw him into a tree like a rag doll.

Orla threw more fireballs at it before it flew at Bradan, talons readied. The creature glared at Orla, and in that short moment, she saw a gleam of something familiar in its eyes. Her fire didn't seem to do much damage to it. She needed a weapon. She conjured a spell in her head, and the tree branches of a nearby tree peeled from the trunk.

The creature could hear the crack of the trees. It flapped its wings and spat a stream of blue fire toward Orla. *Hell!* Orla knew she couldn't get out of this one. She hadn't thought a 'bird' would have the ability to breathe waves of fire. There wasn't enough time for her to dart for cover. She could feel the heat heading toward her.

But just then the fire hit an invisible shield in front of her and bounced off, burning the nearby tree. She saw Bradan lower his arm. So *that* was his talent! He couldn't attack, but he could use some kind of shield to divert the energy elsewhere. The creature turned so fast that Bradan couldn't do anything about it. It flew at him and punctured his chest with its claws.

Bradan fell to the ground, grasping the feet of the creature and pulling it down with him. The tree branch Orla had broken free then became a sharp weapon. She swung her arm, and it stabbed deep into the creature's back. It uttered a horrific quacking noise, flapped its wings, and flew off into the darkness.

Bradan lay on the ground, gasping for air while blood gushed from his chest. Orla helped him up into a sitting position, hoping it would lessen his blood loss. "You fool! If you don't have any skills to protect yourself, why upset that ugly monster? Hang in there. If you die on me, I'll curse you at your grave and all the way to hell."

"I'll end up in hell, will I?" Bradan joked weakly. His head lolled back onto her shoulder, and his consciousness was ebbing.

Orla looked around. They were in the middle of the woods, and there was no way she could carry him back to the village on foot.

The sound of something behind her made her hair stand up.

"Who is that? Don't mess around with me, or I'll burn your ass!" she yelled.

Maeve rushed over to her. "Orla! Thank god it's you. It's so dark, I couldn't tell. I've been following the trail of a dark magic creature all evening and lost their trail . . ."

Orla made a small fireball and lit up a small tree branch on the ground nearby. The light stopped Maeve. "Bradan! What happened to him?"

"Got attacked. Possibly by the same creature you've been following."

"Put him down. Let me see."

"He's lost a lot of blood."

"Can you make more fire?"

Orla nodded and made the fire larger so Macve could see. She opened the front of Bradan's shirt and looked at the wound. "It's not the blood loss that's killing him, it's the poison. That creature—whatever it was—sent poison into his blood."

CHAPTER 16

Orla could see that the blood streaming from Bradan's chest had turned black. Maeve took a small bottle of potion she had in her little bag and tipped it into his mouth.

"Will it cure him?"

Maeve shook her head. "It helps ease the pain. But no, it won't save him."

"So what will?"

"There's a sacred black magic potion in the temple of the clan. That would definitely help, but

they won't give it to anyone. But ask Uncle Daly—
he'll find a way to save his son."

"I'm sorry to tell you this, but he's behind you.
He was torn into pieces by that thing."

"Oh God . . ."

"Who made the potion, and what is it?"

"I think Aunt Anna made it. They're very
secretive about it. It's for the next leader of the
clan."

"So if they want me to lead the clan, will I have
access to the potion?"

"Yes, but you have to swear in."

Orla narrowed her eyes. No one knew she *hadn't*
sworn in with the clan. All the girls who had been
groomed for the position of leader had sworn in on
their first magic lesson. It was a sacred promise
between the individuals and their god. But she
hadn't sworn. That was one of the tricks that had
kept her alive until now. All of her conflicting
emotions and the fact that she would burst into
flame because of them would only work on her if
she had sworn in.

"What are you talking about?" Orla asked
Maeve.

"Come on, you've never sworn in with your clan. I know that."

Orla lowered her voice. "*Nobody* knows."

"You don't suspect me, do you?"

"Nobody knows, Maeve. So what's your plan? What do you want?" Orla backed away.

Tears gleamed in Maeve's eyes. "Come on, don't do this to me, Orla!"

"I could kill you, Maeve, you know that!"

Tears rolled down Maeve's face. "You can do whatever you want to me. Just go get that potion and save Bradan, please!"

Orla looked into Maeve's eyes and mumbled, "You love him, don't you? Does he know that?"

"He's running out of time, Orla, please!"

Orla waved her arms in frustration. "Swearing in . . . that means I have to give up my life—and Lorcan—and stay here forever. How can you be that selfish, Maeve?"

"You can kill me if you want to. I don't care. I've had enough of this place. If you had sworn in, the black magic at the cemetery could have killed you. I knew back then that you hadn't done it. I *am* selfish. If you take the leadership, then Bradan doesn't have to, and then we will have a chance . . ."

"You would trade my life just for a chance with him?"

Maeve shook her head. "You are the rightful leader. You'll have to take that leadership sooner or later, Orla. I don't stand a chance with Bradan, even if he doesn't take the leadership. But I love him. So there, I said it. Do whatever you want."

"You fool! You could have told me," Orla mumbled. "Now you stay here. I'll go get the potion."

"Thank you."

"Don't mention it. But you owe me one."

Maeve nodded through tears.

***

The temple was as mysterious as she remembered it. Orla ducked low behind a stone wall and peeked inside from a distance. She remembered the layout of the temple but still couldn't made an educated guess about where about the potion might be. Her ex-profession as a thief might come in quite handy. She wanted the potion, but she had no intention of swearing anything to the clan.

There was no one around.

Very confident, Orla thought. They thought their magic and spells would protect the temple from thieves, which was probably true. But she was no ordinary thief. She entered the temple. Statues of her gods, ancestral remains, and numerous magical items were placed neatly on the altar. A large picture of a half moon, the symbol of her black magic sorcery clan, was located prominently. They didn't worship the moon, but their gods fed from its negative energy. Half-moon symbols were everywhere in the temple. Orla shook her head and chuckled to herself. Her clan was one third religion, one third magic, and one third emotion. While many magical branches relied on the harmony of the universe—the Ying and Yang and the composite of peaceful elements—what had possessed her ancestors to choose one that was destructive and unnatural? Why had they chosen to forbid love?

She looked around and couldn't see any potion jar or bottle.

Magic lock, she speculated. "Want me to swear in, I will," she said aloud, looking up at her god. She kneeled in front of the altar and stated her oath. It was a life and death statement, a giving-her-soul-to-the-devil kind of swear, and it ought to work, she thought. When Orla opened her eyes and looked up again, a small white bottle of potion was staring down at her from atop the altar.

"Thank you." She smiled and grabbed it. She turned, a quirk at a corner of her mouth appearing, but she quickly squelched it before her ancestors or any mind reader could catch it and strode out of the temple.

She rushed back to the woods. Bradan must have gotten worse as Maeve looked like a mess and was cradling him in her arms. Orla thrust the bottle into Maeve's hand.

"Are you sure it will fix him?" she asked.

Maeve said nothing and flipped the lid open. She nudged his lips open and carefully tipped the contents in. Bradan was white as a sheet. Orla thought he must have died ten times over. But in a short moment, in front of their eyes, he seemed to resume normal breathing.

Maeve laughed as she teared up. "It worked! Oh my god, it worked."

"I can see that, Maeve. Do you want him to know that you begged for his life?"

"What? No!"

"So put him down."

"Oh. Right." Maeve lay Bradan down on the grass. He opened his eyes groggily.

"Oh good, you're awake. Let's get out of here now. I'm freezing," Orla said, looking down at him.

"What happened?" He was still very weak due to the wounds on his chest, but the poison had been counteracted. Maeve shot a frantic look at Orla.

"Bradan, your father died, and you were injured. Remember that?"

Then he recalled. The pain on his face bought tears to Maeve's eyes again. Orla cleared her throat. "I have things I need to do. But first, we have to get you to safety, and it's not going to be the village," Orla declared.

"Why not?"

"Whatever attacked you knew you had left the village for the woods. Someone in the village tipped it off."

Bradan closed his eyes and seemed to agree with what she said. Orla continued, "You should stay with Maeve."

"What?" Bradan tried to sit up but flopped down again.

"You need to be taken care of. Nobody would guess you'd stay with her. Maeve, would you mind?"

"Yes, I mean no. Of course not. No one in the village knows my current place."

Orla and Maeve helped Bradan up. Orla saw no way out of helping Maeve taking Bradan to her place. He was still too weak to walk by himself. It took the two of them, flanking his sides, and they still had to walk one slow step at a time.

Orla looked up to the sky and saw a crack of dawn beginning to show itself. She sighed and thought of Lorcan.

CHAPTER 17

Keeva's scream sent Lorcan springing to his feet. He glanced down and saw that his chest had healed completely. Lorcan knew that Keeva slept innocently and deeply and would never remember ordinary dreams. But her nightmares were of the worst kind. Similar to her ability to sense death, her nightmares were all about death, and they were frighteningly accurate. Storming into Keeva's bedroom, he saw her sitting in bed and shaking, with tears streaming down her face.

Lorcan jumped onto the bed and pulled his sister into his arms to soothe her, but she backed away from him.

Her eyes were devastated, and she backed further away. What had she seen in her nightmare? Whose death? "Keeva, talk to me," he said gently, but she kept shaking her head.

Riley and Noah arrived at the door. Lorcan acknowledged them, then glanced back at Keeva. He vaguely remembered asking for Riley in his delirium last night. He remembered asking him to perform the surgery to remove the bullet.

"Thanks for coming," Lorcan said. Riley nodded, his eyes trained on the shaking Keeva.

Noah ran in and flew into Lorcan's arms. As he hugged Lorcan, Noah whispered into his ear, "She sees dead people. She dreams about them, too."

Lorcan eased Noah out of his arms and looked at his face, then he looked back at Keeva. "I know, Noah. I know about her visions and dreams."

Noah looked at Keeva, then in front of an astonished Lorcan and Riley, he climbed onto the bed and curled into Keeva's arms. Keeva embraced him as tears rolled down her face.

"Why don't you tell them what you saw? When I talked to Dad, it helped," Noah said.

Keeva shook her head. "I can't . . ."

"Do you mind if I tell them what you saw? I think Uncle Lorcan should know."

Lorcan stood up, bracing for the news. Riley flopped to the reading chair and put his head in his hands.

Keeva nodded to Noah. Noah turned around. "Uncle Lorcan, I think Keeva and I had the same dream. We saw each other in our dreams. We saw a big bird, blood, body parts and . . . Orla."

Lorcan braced his hands against the wall and inhaled deeply. Then he turned around and asked, "Did you see whose body parts they were?"

Noah shook his head. "It was dark. I saw Orla's face . . ."

"I need to see her," Lorcan muttered and charged out the door.

He thundered down the hallway. Keeva, Riley, and Noah chased after him. The lights in the house flickered, and a wave of fresh and lively air washed through the entire house. The eerie silence suddenly lifted, and they heard the hum of the forest and the wind. Birds flapped their wings, fighting for the small birdbath Keeva had made for them. Insects orchestrated soothing Irish country songs. And people chattered.

People? Lorcan came to a skidding halt and turned back. Keeva looked at him. They both heard the familiar sound of people in the house. Riley frowned at their expressions as they rushed down the stairs.

In the front garden, a man was holding a large plant trimmer, enjoying the birds in competition for a place in the bath. He turned and saw the group of people. "Keeva, your bath is very popular with the birds. I told you. Soon you will regret it because they make a lot of noise." He pointed at Lorcan. "And who might this be?"

"This is my brother, Lorcan, and his friends from England, Riley and Noah," Keeva said quickly and scurried after Lorcan as he made his way down the corridor toward the kitchen.

There were greeted there by the aroma of his favorite lemon and almond cake and the sight of his mother giving instructions to the chef. Lorcan's legs carried him into kitchen. His mind was numb with confusion.

His mother looked at him with her soft green eyes, which gleamed with tears of joy when she saw him. She opened her arms wide. Lorcan rushed in and embraced her, almost lifting her off her feet. She released him and cupped his face with her hands.

"Look at you, you're tired." Then she rubbed his back warmly. "How are your injuries?"

"I'm okay, Mother." Lorcan smiled. His mother had no memories of what had happened after he'd run into her arms with claw wounds on his back a few days ago. Keeva walked into the kitchen and stared at the chef—the same chef she'd seen dead on the floor. The chef frowned at the tears on Keeva's face.

"What happened, Keeva? Are you okay, sweetheart? Why are you crying?"

His mother approached Keeva and wiped the tears from her face. Keeva was dumbstruck and couldn't say a thing. Riley and Noah stepped into the kitchen.

"This is my friend Riley and his son Noah," Lorcan said. "This is my mother."

Riley nodded a greeting. "Nice to meet you, Mrs. Brody. Lorcan has talked about you a lot."

"Call me Jane." She smiled. "Have you just arrived? Stay with us for a while. There are plenty of beautiful sights to see. I'm sure Noah would enjoy it."

Riley was about to say something, but Lorcan cut in. "We'll go for a walk in the woods, Mother."

"That's a good idea," Jane said. "Come home early for brunch."

Lorcan nodded and strode out. Riley and Keeva rushed after him. Riley turned at Noah. "You stay at home, Noah. Don't say anything to anyone before I figure out what's going on. Can you promise me?"

Noah pouted, but then nodded.

CHAPTER 18

At the edge of the woods, Lorcan turned around. "I broke the curse on my parents, and as a result, Orla died. Is that what this is all about? Is that what you saw, Keeva?"

"No. I don't know . . . You don't know that Orla is dead."

"What curse?" Riley asked.

"You don't need to know, Riley. But I need to see for myself." Lorcan turned around and hurried away. He tore through the forest like it was nothing, breaking through the tall grasses and young trees as he ran blindly.

He had no idea where Orla's house was, but he followed his instinct. There was a familiar trail of her scent in the air, and he followed it. He didn't know when his sense had become that developed, but he could feel every delicate scent and sound around him. He kept running.

And there it was. He stopped just inside the treeline, looking into the gardens behind Orla's house. He stood there, hidden in the foliage, as Orla walked out into the garden followed by a woman. She was alive. Lorcan was deliriously happy. She was walking and talking there, right in front of him. But how could he know that this wasn't just another illusion? Lorcan stepped out and entered the garden.

Orla saw him, and tears immediately poured down her face.

"Lorcan! You're alive!" She ran toward him but was held back by the woman behind her.

"Stop right there or you'll kill her!" the woman yelled at him, and that stopped him in his tracks.

"Let me go, Alana!" Orla protested. Alana was the same size as Orla, but for some reason she appeared to be incredibly strong. Orla couldn't free herself from her grip and appeared to weaken by the second. Her eyes reddened, and he could see the vein on her forehead begin to throb. She grunted in pain. When Alana released her, she fell to the ground.

Lorcan charged toward Orla, but Alana warned him again. "She's sworn in with the clan and will be their leader. If she keeps thinking about you, she'll burst into flames."

Lorcan could see a shade of the fire in Orla's eyes. He withdrew, backing up so quickly that he almost fell on his backside. "Knock her out, Alana! Please!" he yelled.

"If you don't want her to think about you, don't come here."

"Lorcan, don't leave me!" Orla called out, lying on the grass. Her eyes glassed over.

"I'm sorry, Orla," Lorcan said and ran away as fast as he could, but he could still hear her whispering, "Lorcan, take me home. Don't leave me. Take me home with you . . ."

Lorcan ran and ran, not realizing that tears were streaming down his face. He'd lost her—not in death, but in life. Which one was worse, he couldn't say. He collided with Riley, and both fell to the ground.

Riley stood up. "What the heck, Lorcan?"

Keeva approached, panting. As Lorcan stood , Keeva pointed behind them, shaking. When he turned around, he saw the yellow wolf that he'd fought before. He faced it, putting his arms out in front of him and showing the beast he was unarmed. The wolf's eyes darted back and forth from his hands to his face, then to his friend and sister, searching for the biggest threat.

"I don't know why you're here, but I'm not going to shift, and I'm not going to fight you, either, unless you attack my companions." The wolf cocked its head like it was listening to what he had to say. It then hunched low to the ground, preparing to spring. Lorcan didn't move, and the wolf launched its heavy body into the air. When it landed, its front paws were on Lorcan's chest, and it closed its jaws on his throat.

Keeva screamed, and Riley dove forward to help, but Lorcan used his hands to wave them away. Obediently, they moved away, and then Lorcan lay still, arms flat on the ground, not fighting at all. The wolf's heavy breath made little eddies of dirt swirl near his ear, but still he didn't move. The wolf gently let go of his throat and backed up a little so it could see Lorcan's face. Lorcan just stared back at it, not trying to be intimidating or anything of the sort, just staring. The wolf climbed off of him and ran off, disappearing back into the green foliage of the forest.

For a few minutes, no one moved. No one made a sound. Then Riley came over and helped Lorcan to his feet. Lorcan had just opened his mouth to thank Riley for his help when Riley pulled back an arm with a fist attached and let it fly. His fist connected Lorcan's cheek with a satisfying crack, and Lorcan fell to the ground once more.

"You're pathetic, Lorcan. You wanted that dog to rip your throat out, didn't you?"

This time it was Keeva who helped Lorcan to his feet, but as soon as he was up, she yanked her hand back. Lorcan looked into her face and saw the same anger he had heard clearly in Riley's voice, maybe tempered with a little fear.

"Today is not a good day to die. I have lots of things to do. I admit, it was pathetic. You got your punch in, are you happy now?"

Riley threw his arms in the air in frustration.

Lorcan continued. "I just saw Orla. She's alive."

"That's good, isn't it?" Keeva asked in a shaky voice.

"I'm sorry if I scared you. After I found out that Orla can never be with me if she wants to remain alive, and after I saw her running toward me even knowing the consequences, I wanted to let that wolf tear my throat out. I just couldn't think straight."

"What's the news?" Riley asked.

"Orla asked me not to leave her and to take her home. She would fight to the death for what she wants, and she's definitely not the kind to leave a dying wish."

Riley chuckled. "Couldn't agree more. So that's a hint then."

Lorcan nodded. "A way out for us, I think. I just have to figure out how to get there."

Lorcan turned and headed home with Keeva trailing behind. "Don't you feel the need to fill me in at all?" she said. "I met your girlfriend for the first time a couple of days ago, and Riley gets to know a load more stuff about your life out there." Keeva pointed at Riley.

"And he suffered for it, Keeva." Lorcan smiled and ruffled Keeva's hair. "Okay, for both of you—the condensed version is that Orla is a sorceress."

"What?" Keeva asked incredulously.

"Just accept it—*if* you want the rest of the story. Her family uses black magic and won't allow her to be with me. To save me, she made a promise to return to her family. Then she broke her promise, and we ran away together. We currently live and work at a place that you could say is . . . off planet."

"You're alien? I thought you were a werefox," Keeva said.

"I'll take the alien theory," Riley said and pulled out a piece of paper from his pocket. "I tested your blood last night in my portable lab. Only half of your DNA is human."

Lorcan cocked an eyebrow. "And what's the other half?"

"I need a more sophisticated machine to analyze that result," Riley answered.

"What about werefox?" Keeva asked. "I saw you turn into one."

"Werefoxes are mythical creatures, Keeva, and I don't understand their makeup. But even the werefoxes say I'm not one of them. On a mission in

Japan, I was bitten by a one, and the next thing I knew, I could turn into one and could heal my wounds quickly, as you've already seen."

"You make it sound too simple, Lorcan. And you left out the part that you nearly died a few times before heading off to that outer space place," Riley said.

Keeva turned, looking at Lorcan, her eyes welling up. "And you didn't tell me or our parents any of that! Didn't it ever occur in your brain that we're your family, and we care for you, regardless of where you are and what you are?" She stormed away.

Lorcan glared at Riley. "Did you need to stir that up?"

"It's a fact, that's life. She needs to know life out there is tough. Your life is hard and not cushy like hers. She thinks the last few days is proof that she's grown up and mature. She thinks having some psychic connections to Noah make her understand him more than I do, and that she can pass judgment on me and tell me how to raise my son . . ."

A clump of dirt hit on Riley's chest.

"Hey!" he yelled.

Keeva picked up more dirt and grass and kept throwing. "Now that you've fixed my brother, you can pack up your stuff, your kid, your cat, and your life and get the hell out of my head!" she yelled back.

"I have no intention of getting into your head given how muddy it is with all that psychic stuff. I have enough to worry about!"

"Hey! Stop it, you two. I have a curse to break. We have a life and death matter here. And you're going nowhere, Riley. I need your help." Lorcan pointed at his sister. "And you, young lady, I need you to help take care of Mother. Can you do that?"

Keeva glared at Riley and turned on her heel, stomping away. They all headed home.

CHAPTER 19

The heat was eating up her brain. Orla didn't know it would hurt so much. She had sworn in at the temple in order to get the potion for Bradan. But she thought she'd had it covered and had tricked her gods. She had sworn to death if she loved any man who hated her family on Earth. And Lorcan didn't hate her family. He had a temper, and he could kill. But he wasn't capable of hate. So it couldn't be her swearing in that was hurting her at the moment.

She wondered if Lorcan had gotten her hint. They understood each other, but given the situation, he might not be able to think straight. She needed him to take her out of here and back to the Daimon Gate and Eudaiz. She needed him. He had to be able to see through the haze of the pain and confusion.

How had she ended up back here? She had left Bradan in the woods with Maeve and had gone for Lorcan. What had happened next? She tried to remember, but her mind kept coming back blank. Then she recalled it. It was the wolf. A gigantic yellow wolf had knocked her out and had taken her back here. When she woke up, Alana was looming over her, ranting about how she had gotten out under Alana's watch again, making her look like a fool. Orla lied to Alana and said she'd gone out for fresh air and had gotten lost. She knew the excuse was lame, but Alana accepted it and didn't ask any more questions.

Orla tried to stand up, but her legs buckled and she fell to the floor. Alana cursed and helped her up.

"I want to go and get some help for you, Orla. Get Bradan and Uncle Daly. But I have no confidence that you won't run away again, even in your current condition. So I'm going to call Bradan's cell phone again, and hopefully he'll answer this time," Alana said, wagging her finger at Orla, warning her not to make a move.

She dialed and tapped her finger impatiently on the table next to the phone. "I'm going to get you a doctor, so sit still, Orla." Alana warned her again. "Damn it, Bradan doesn't pick up his cell. What's the point of having it?" Alana slammed the phone down.

Orla stood up again and staggered toward the door. "Sit down." Alana grabbed her from behind, but Orla elbowed her. Alana roared in pain, pulled Orla's hair, and slapped her so hard that they both fell on the floor.

Orla saw stars. The pain in her head was so unbearable that she could feel her life leaving her. She didn't know why her protective spells weren't working.

Maeve walked in and rushed over to help her up. "Are you okay?" Then she turned to Alana and asked, "What did you do to her?"

Alana stood with hands on her hips. "What did *I* do to *her*? I tried to help, and she hit me. What's wrong with her—apart from the obvious?"

"She's in agony. Can't you see that?" Maeve raised her voice.

"I'm the one in agony. I've had enough of this. I'll call the aunties and uncles, and they can come over and sort this out. And you? They won't be happy seeing you here, Maeve."

Orla's eyes were almost rolled up entirely in her head. She could feel someone using dark magic on her, but she was too weak and in too much pain to cast her protective spell.

"Why is she in so much pain?" Maeve asked.

"Ask her boyfriend. If I were her best friend, as you claim you are, I'd go and tell him to stay away," Alana said.

Orla leaned back in the chair and closed her eyes. She heard Maeve whispering in her mind, the way they had always communicated. *"Are you in physical pain, or is this the work of black magic?"*

"It's the magic. I need to raise my protective shield. The pain is stopping me," Orla responded in her mind.

"I thought you were going to find Lorcan?" Maeve asked.

"I did, but something attacked me on the way. I think it was a wolf. The next thing I knew, I was

lying here in the front yard. Then Alana found me and took me inside," Orla responded, then asked, *"Why are you here?"*

"I sensed shapeshifters in your direction just after you left, so I went to check on you."

Orla appeared to be resting with her eyes closed. Maeve pulled out a small bottle.

"Hey, what are you doing? She isn't going to take any of your white magic potion," Alana said.

"There's no magic in this, just pure medicine to help with the pain."

"I don't know that. And I don't know you. Everyone will be furious with me. Bradan and Uncle Daly will be so pissed." Alana approached and pulled Maeve away from Orla.

"You don't even want to know why I'm here?" Maeve asked.

"I don't care. Now get out of this house. I've called everyone. They'll eat you alive."

Maeve put Bradan's and Daly's chain necklaces on the table. They were unique symbolic clan items that only left their persons when they were dead. Alana stared at the items and froze. Taking advantage of Alana's distraction, Maeve poured the potion into Orla's mouth.

The medicine was like liquid gold. Orla could feel it wash through her system and her mind and ease the pain. She wished she could have a fraction of Maeve's skills in natural medicine.

"Are they dead?" Alana's voice shook.

"I'm sorry Alana, but yes. I found them, or what was left of them, in the woods."

Tears flopped down on Alana's face. "Oh God, oh my God." She walked back and forth, raking her hands through her hair. Orla glanced at Maeve, and they signaled each other and both stormed out of the door at once.

"Hey!" Alana yelled after them. In the front garden, Orla sensed a wedge of energy. "It's too late, they're here already. You go, Maeve. If you get to see Lorcan, tell him to get me out of here. As long as I am off this planet and with him, we'll be fine."

She pushed Maeve away before she could protest. As soon as Orla turned back, the entire family had flooded the front yard. Alana rushed out from the house. "She was trying to run again!" she cried. "Maeve helped her. It wasn't my fault. The two of them are wicked."

"Be quiet, Alana. Your only job was to guard her, and look at what happened," Aunt Anna scolded.

"Come on, she's young and inexperienced. And our up and coming leader is not exactly an innocent soul." Uncle Tony chuckled and wrapped his arm around Orla's shoulder. "Let's get you inside the house so we can talk."

Orla knew the arm around her shoulders wasn't there for protection. Uncle Tony hadn't seemed to like Uncle Daly much when she saw them a few nights ago, but she had a feeling that he wasn't exactly happy about their deaths, either."

Alana stood watching as he escorted Orla back into the house. Her lips trembled, and tears gleamed in her eyes. For the first time, Orla felt sorry for her. Her life here must be horrible. Orla wondered why she didn't leave when she had a chance.

CHAPTER 20

Maeve ran as fast as she could back to her place. It wasn't exactly a mansion, but it was protected and blessed by love and cared for by her mother. It was comfortable enough. But now, apart from bringing back the memories of her mother, the house didn't give her much. There had been countless times Maeve wondered what kept her here.

Her mother had said she could leave at any time—go to a large city, make friends, have a life.

Didn't she have a life? Maybe she didn't. Bradan had entered her life and left her defenseless. She had met him at the village festival, one of those events that didn't discriminate against religion or theological belief. Then she'd found out he was her very distant cousin from the black magic clan. And with that knowledge came the end of her dream. Bradan was a black magic sorcerer. She was a white witch. She thought her devotion to her God could do her good. But what she had gotten instead was a joke of faith.

Maeve stormed into the bedroom. Well, it was her bedroom, but she let Bradan sleep in it, and she slept on the couch in the living room. She touched his forehead and found that his fever was gone. Before she could withdraw her hand, he grabbed it.

"I was just checking your temperature, Bradan."

He let go her hand.

"I'll bring some food and water for you. The medicine and the instructions are on the table. Can you take care of that yourself?"

"Where are you going?"

"Someone in your clan wanted you dead. I let the news out to see who would do the happy dance."

"Where's Orla?"

"She's stuck. She was going to Lorcan's, but they caught her. No—she said a wolf got her and took her back. Now I have to go to Lorcan to ask him to get her out of there."

"The full moon is getting closer. If they think I'm dead, then they'll hang on very tightly to Orla. Getting her out isn't going to be easy."

"They should be happy. She's sworn in. They'll think they can hold her. That she dare not run away."

"She swore in? What the fuck?"

Maeve stared at Bradan. "I always thought it was required. Something you did at a very young age."

"It is, but I didn't do it, either. That's why my father was so upset in the woods. He wanted me to swear in before the full moon. We argued, and the next thing I knew, he was dead. And now it's Orla . . . why did she do that?"

"The claws from that monster bird has poisoned your blood. I told Orla that the potion in the temple was the only solution."

Bradan banged his head back down on the pillow. "And she had to swear in to get it! Fuck! Fuck! Fuck!" He punctuated the curses with the banging of his head.

140

"That's not very helpful, Bradan! Is there a way out of this?"

"Someone has to love her enough to take the challenge."

"What kind of challenge?"

"It's not possible, so don't ask."

"Just tell me."

"Maeve, no one is going to love anyone enough to do such a stupid thing."

"Is that what you really believe?"

"I am a black magic sorcerer, what do you want me to say?"

"If that's what you believe, why didn't you swear in when you were a kid?"

"As long as I'm here, as long as I'm with the family, that's what I am going to do. I will do the right thing, regardless of whether I believe it will work or not."

"If that's your plan, why argue with your father?"

Bradan turned to face the wall.

"Bradan!"

"Please leave me alone, Maeve."

"All right. But answer one last question. What would you have done if Orla hadn't come back this time?"

Silence.

"Bradan, we risked our lives to save you. We deserve an answer."

Bradan turned back and looked at her. "I would run, Maeve. I would do what Orla did years ago. That was always my plan. That's why my father was so upset."

She waved her arms in the air and was about to spit out a sarcastic remark, but then she realized she didn't have grounds. She let her hands flop to her sides. "Fair enough. If she hadn't come back, in a few days you would have just disappeared . . . would have run away from your black magic family. Oh God . . . I wasted my whole life . . ."

"Excuse me?"

"Don't worry. You don't have to run any more as Orla will take the shit for you. I have to get to Lorcan. We'll figure something out to save Orla. Take care of yourself. There's plenty of food in the house."

Maeve turned to leave. She heard Bradan try to get off the bed but fall back down again. She locked the door from the outside and left.

PART TWO

CHAPTER 21

As soon as Keeva walked through their front gate, she staggered back a few steps. Riley grabbed her elbow to support. She shrugged him off, but his grip was firm. "Are you okay?" Riley gazed into her eyes.

"What's wrong, Keeva?" Lorcan asked.

She shook her head. "Just feeling uneasy. I don't know what it is . . ."

"If you have a vision, I want you to tell me. Promise?" Lorcan asked. Keeva nodded.

Then she dropped to her knees, breathing heavily, and tears started streaming down her face. Lorcan reached for her, but Riley pushed him aside. Riley held Keeva, rubbing her back up and down and rocking her, exactly the way he'd done to Noah. "Take it easy. Deep breaths. There you go. Calm down, Keeva. It will pass."

She was gasping, and she nuzzled into Riley's chest as he kept caressing her back, but she couldn't calm down.

"What do you see, Keeva?" Lorcan asked.

"Nothing. I can't see anything." Tears streamed down her face, and at the same time, pain stabbed at Lorcan's chest. He knew it had to be bad news.

"Keeva?" he called her gently.

"Don't push her," Riley scolded.

"I can't see, Lorcan. I know it's bad, but I can't see." Keeva freed herself from Riley's hold and darted into the house. Jane walked out of the kitchen and saw Keeva, but before she could ask anything, Keeva charged past her and ran toward Noah's room.

In the guest room, Noah sat in the corner of the bed with tears glistening in his eyes. Aris sat next to him, meowing noisily. Keeva held Noah's hands.

"Did you see anything? You saw more than me, right? Noah, please!"

Noah looked at Riley who had just entered the room. Riley nodded. Noah squeezed Keeva's hands. "I saw your father. I'm sorry."

"Oh God," Keeva cried out loud. "How? Where? That must be why he didn't answer his phone all night."

"Is he dead?" Lorcan asked.

"I don't know." Noah answered.

"Can you tell where he is?" Lorcan asked.

Noah shook his head. "It was dark. There were rocks . . . and water. He was in his car."

Noah looked up and toward the door. Everyone turned to see Jane standing in the doorway. She was quiet, and she didn't ask for an explanation. Jane contemplated and then said, "The cliffs. He's at the cliffs."

"It's a very large area if he drove back from town that way," Lorcan said.

Aris meowed louder and then began to hiss until he got some attention. Noah looked at the kitten, then he looked at everyone and said, "Aris knows where to find him."

***

The winter breeze cut into his skin. But Lorcan couldn't feel much. The cliff was high and steep. Any car slipping off the country road and dropping down there wouldn't have a chance of survival. His father, as far as he knew, didn't have any special ability with which to heal himself.

Pain pounded in his chest. Every vein in his head throbbed—it was the agony of loss and fear. What had he said to his father last time they spoke? He couldn't remember. He had been on the verge of passing out after being hit by the bullet.

Lorcan's eyes were glued on the kitten, who strode straight ahead in front of them. The others were saying something, but Lorcan wasn't paying attention. He cursed silently. He needed to find his father. It would be his fault if he died. His father wouldn't agree, but hell, they never agreed on anything.

Aris stopped in front of a puddle. There was a fresh skid mark in the mud. He followed the track to the edge of the cliff and saw his father's car teetering on a rock ledge twenty feet down. The ledge wasn't too far down from where they stood, but from there downward, it seemed like an endless drop.

CHAPTER 22

Lorcan turned, angled himself, and began to climb down. Riley pulled at him. "Don't! Let me call for help," Riley said.

"It'll be too late. With this wind, the car will slip off the rock at any second," Lorcan said and continued his descent.

"You can't hold the car back with your bare hands!"

"I'll pull him out."

"That's crazy, Lorcan!"

He ignored Riley and kept climbing down. It didn't take him long to reach the ledge. It was large enough to hold maybe half a car and maybe four people. He could see his father trapped in the dangling car.

"Father!"

His father opened his eyes and turned to look at him. He blinked a few times as if to make sure it was really Lorcan who was standing beside the car.

"Hang on, Father, I'm going to get you out. Can you undo your seatbelt?" he asked as he approached the car to open the door.

"Don't touch it! It'll fall!" Ferris waved Lorcan away, and his slight movement rocked the car.

"No, no, don't move, Father—just unbuckle your seatbelt for me."

Lorcan heard a sound behind him and saw Riley jump down onto the rock behind him. Lorcan could see his father release the seatbelt then lean toward the passenger side. The car rocked even more.

"Don't move, Father! Stay still!" Lorcan approached and gingerly grabbed the door handle. His father sat straight up, holding a small red box in his hand and reached out the broken window to hand it to Lorcan.

"Take this, son."

The car rocked more and slipped a bit. The handle slipped out of Lorcan's grasp.

"Don't move!"

"Take the box," Ferris scolded and thrust the box out. The car slid more with his movement.

"All right, all right." Lorcan grabbed the box and tossed it to Riley. Then he grabbed the handle and yanked the door open. The car was tipped precariously at the edge. Lorcan grabbed his father's arm.

"Let go of me, Lorcan. The hand brake broke and bent when the car went over the cliff and landed here. It pierced me—I'm stuck with the car. Don't hang on to me. You'll be dragged down, too."

Lorcan lifted the side of his father's jacket and saw that the handbrake had pinned him to his seat.

"I'll get you out of there." Lorcan grabbed his father's shoulders. The car started to tip.

"Let go!" his father yelled.

"No!" Lorcan pulled at his father.

"Don't do this, Lorcan."

The car rocked and rocked and slipped even further.

Riley braced himself against the rock and grabbed hold of Lorcan's belt from behind. Lorcan yanked his father out of the car just before it dropped into the nothingness below. Papers flew out from inside the car, floating in the air and raining down to the bottom of the gully.

Blood was everywhere.

Lorcan had his father half on and half off the rock ledge, and he could see a large gash on his father's stomach which extended all the way up to his chest. He pulled his father up into the safety of his arms. "We're going to get you up. Mother is waiting for you. And you're lucky—we have a doctor handy. Riley!" Lorcan called out. Riley inched forward but said nothing.

"Say something, will you?" Lorcan asked.

"I'm afraid there's nothing I can do. This is too much damage, Lorcan . . ."

"You can help him. You're a good doctor. Please . . ."

Ferris opened his eyes. "The box . . ."

"Here!" Riley handed it over quickly.

His father looked at him with the eyes of a dying man. "You never belonged here, Lorcan . . . Your mother and I needed you . . . she loves you too

154

much . . . I love you too much . . . we broke our promise . . ."

"Please don't talk. I'll take you to the hospital."

"We called the paramedics. They're coming," Riley said.

Ferris smiled weakly. "I've lived long enough. I wanted a child for your mother, but I had no idea of the consequences. I signed up for the project, but I thought it was just a scientific experiment. It was too late when I found out it was extraterrestrial. They took half of my DNA and with the other half they created . . . Your profile and your special abilities were documented on the papers in the car . . ."

"I don't care."

"You should, Lorcan. We were supposed to have you for only ten years. But your mother couldn't let you go, so we didn't give you back. When you took off with Orla, we thought it might be for the best. We would rather lose you, knowing you were safe on Earth and being human, than let them take you."

Tears rolled down Lorcan's face.

"The tears and the emotions are the human part of you. Treasure them, Lorcan. I don't know what the other part will do to those things, but I know you're special. You have several powerful abilities . . ."

"You didn't want to give me back, so now they decide to kill you?"

"Keeping my promise will save me. If I had pressed the button inside the red box, they would have done whatever I wanted within their power. But I don't need that. All I need is your mother, you, and Keeva . . ."

"Can they save you now if I press it?"

"No. I broke my promise, and that was the end of that deal . . . But that red box is my only connection to them. You are their subject, and they will save you, whatever it takes. I wasn't sure you'd survive the bullet at the house, so I went to retrieve the box . . ."

They heard the sound of the rescue helicopter hovering in the air.

"Father, you're going to be fine."

"Take care of your mother and Keeva, Lorcan."

"No, that's *your* job. You said I don't belong here."

"I'm afraid I can't do it anymore. Press the button in the box and find out your origin, but please try to maintain contact with your mother and sister. You're all they have now . . ." He closed his eyes to catch his breath.

"One more thing . . . I didn't drive off the road . . . There was a large puma . . . It jumped out right in front of the car . . ." he trailed off, and then he was gone.

"No, no! Don't die, don't leave me!" The pain was unbearable – as if he was losing a part of his soul. This was the family he had always taken for granted. Now he'd just learned that it had never really been his. Something was tearing at his heart. It hurt. He wagered the human part of him was reacting to the situation.

The other part of him was heating up. Whatever it was, it was eating at him right now. Uncontrollable. He saw sparks of electrical waves in front of him. The energy surging inside him was unstoppable. More sparks and energy erupted everywhere like lightning in a storm. He heard Riley said something, ask him not to do something.

What was he talking about?

The air around him was chaotic. His mind was a mess. The helicopter hovered, but was being flung back and forth in the air as if it were a toy dangling from a rope in the wind. He heard the others yelling from the top of the cliff, and he could make out shouting coming from the helicopter and from Riley behind him.

Was he sending out that electric current again?

He looked around and saw large patches of rocks tumbling from the cliffs nearby.

More yelling. Were they yelling at him?

The helicopter approached. He watched as a wave of electric current hit it. There was screaming as it spun and dove downward. But then the chopper regained balance and flew back up again. Lorcan realized it must be him. But he couldn't control the electric current emanating from him. Riley called out again for him to stop.

He turned to tell Riley he hadn't done anything, and all saw was Riley staggering back and rolling off the edge, hanging on to the ledge by his fingertips. In a haze of confusion, he grabbed Riley's hands and hoisted him back onto the rock.

"Look away from me!" Riley shouted.

Lorcan didn't understand, but he obeyed. He turned away, facing his back to Riley. More patches of rocks at a distance where his eyes landed thundered down the cliffs. He felt a punch at his temple from behind, and then the world went black.

CHAPTER 23

Orla worked her mind frantically for a way out of the situation. She had sent Maeve to Lorcan with the message, but she couldn't totally rely on that. Lorcan might have gotten the hint from her before, but to act on it wouldn't be easy. He didn't have any experience in doing magic, and he didn't know the lay of the land in her part of the woods at all.

Uncle Tony seemed to be the one in charge now that Uncle Daly was gone. There were countless of others in the family that she didn't recognize or remember. They sat quietly in the house, waiting for Tony's instructions. Her magic class had had several kids, but the elite group had only a handful groomed for the leadership position. Now that she recalled , Bradan hadn't been in the elite group at all. But he was second in line after her.

How had this leadership line-up been determined? she wondered.

"We have only six days until the full moon. We can't afford any mistakes, or it will be another ten years of waiting," Tony said. "We don't have a choice now that Bradan is gone—we have only Orla." He turned toward her. "I'm sorry, Orla, we don't want to be rough on you, but I hope you understand the situation. You do have a track record of running away."

"What will happen if you don't have me?" she asked.

"We don't even want to consider that possibility now, dear," Aunt Anna said.

"I don't want this, so I'm going to be a very bad leader—or even worse, do something that harms the family!" Orla said.

Tony chuckled. "Thanks for pointing that out. But don't worry. You don't have to manage anything."

Orla narrowed her eyes. "You just want a puppet leader? Maybe a sacrificial lamb?"

Tony laughed. "You can choose to be a puppet if you don't want to be involved or you're lacking in talent. As far as being a sacrificial lamb, don't worry, we don't kill our own."

"What exactly does the position require?" Tony glanced at Anna, and then back at Orla. She continued, "I'm entitled to know. You should know by now that I'm stubborn, and I have nothing to lose here."

Tony nodded. "All right. You're going to know sooner or later. This full moon is not like any others. This is the cycle when the full energy will be loaded onto the current leader. And of course, it will later be distributed to us."

"You want me to serve as a vessel?"

"You will be a pure channel to receive the power from our God. You will be powerful, and you should consider it an honor."

"What if I keep the power to myself?"

"You will always keep the power. Part of the power will be transferred to us via ceremonies because we are family, but the transfer will not weaken you as it doesn't take anything from you."

Orla smiled. "You will receive the power, as long as I stay with the family forever, right?"

"Yes. That's the one condition. I'm glad we are coming to an understanding."

Orla smiled. "I'm afraid I can't help you with the mission. I'm no longer a part of this family. If I receive the power, I will not be transferring to you naturally."

A few uncles and aunts stood up, and the room hummed with discussion.

"What do you mean?"

"I was married to Lorcan in front of God. I belong to him and to his family. You can give me the power if you like, but you know where it will be transferred."

Tony's face turned red. "Why did you marry a man you don't love?"

"I love Lorcan."

Tony swung his arm, and a beam of fire hit the ceilings, burning a large hole. "If you love him, and you married him, you would be dead. Either you lied to us just now, or you didn't swear in!"

A young man sneaked into the room and whispered something into Anna's ear. "Hold on," Anna interrupted before Tony continued his rant.

"The potion is missing," Anna said.

"What potion?" Tony asked.

"The one at the temple. The *one*."

Tony's hiss was audible. "It wasn't in plain sight. Only the entitled can see it." He fired a deadly look at Orla. "You took it?"

"I took what?" Orla asked.

"You took the potion from the temple. The one for the ceremony," Tony growled.

"I don't even know what it is—why would I take it?"

Tony roared and blasted another stream of fire into the wall. "I can make another one," Anna said.

"There's not enough time," Tony roared again and paced the floor.

"I said I can make it—if I go now, and if you can handle the other housekeeping matters." Anna shot a look at Orla and scurried to the door. Chatter filled the room.

"Quiet!" Tony demanded. The noise died down instantly.

"How can I be sure that you were married in front of God," Tony asked Orla.

"You can't. But you can risk it and go through with the ceremony and see if the power is transferred to Lorcan's family."

"Someone has to ask Lorcan to denounce their marriage in front of our God at the temple," Tony said.

"I can do it," Alana said from the corner. "I don't want to be her warden. I'll deliver the message for you."

"You do know that you have to cross to *that* side of the woods to do it, right?" Tony asked.

"I know." Alana bit her lip slightly. "Can I take a man with me for protection?"

Tony shrugged and pointed to a tall man standing next to the window. "Sam, go with her." Then he turned back to Alana. "Tell Lorcan to be at the temple tomorrow at noon—or else." Then he moved toward Orla. She maintained a stern stare. In a flash, she saw Tony's hand come at her, and then the whole world went black.

CHAPTER 24

Lorcan groggily opened his eyes and saw the blurry ceiling and the headboard of the bed looming over him. Images of furniture and other decorative items floated in the air, flickered, and then settled. He blinked to clear his vision. His limbs didn't seem to belong to him, and each of his movements felt as if he was trying to move a mountain.

He remembered it now—the incident at the cliffs, the death of his father, and what his father had said before he died.

He was officially an orphan.

He must have drained all of his energy in electric waves at the cliffs in a haze of confusion and emotional pain. His human subconscious and the other part of him were tangled in a gigantic mess. He felt a tug at his hand and found Aris licking it.

"Thank you, Aris," he muttered. The door slid open and Noah walked in with a glass of water.

Lorcan smiled. "Since when can you read my mind, Noah?"

Lorcan sat up and gratefully took the water from him. The boy climbed onto the bed and hugged him. "I'm sorry about your father."

Lorcan held Noah in his arms and rubbed his back. "Me, too. Where is everyone?"

"Downstairs. Your mother and Keeva just got back from wherever they went to make arrangements for your father. Keeva was okay. She didn't cry much."

"Where's your father?"

"He's with Keeva. Glued to her. He said he had to keep an eye on her. Showing support and all that. But I know he likes her."

"And do you mind that, Noah?"

"Mind what?"

"If Keeva took the place of your mother, would you mind that?"

Noah shook his head. "No one will take the place of my mother. She's in heaven. But I think Keeva saw my mother, and they might have an agreement between them for her to take care of my father."

Lorcan chuckled. "Now you're weirding me out . . . What happened at the cliffs?"

"You shot something from your eyes—like a machine gun or something. It took down a lot of rocks on the cliffs and some trees, and you would've shot down the helicopter if my father hadn't knocked you out. I think he told the rescue people that you and he were trying to stop a special weapon that had automatically discharged. He said the weapon had belonged to your father, but it went over the cliffs."

Lorcan raised an eyebrow. "They bought that story?"

Noah shrugged. "They must have. It was chaotic. Stuff was flying everywhere, and it was foggy. Nobody saw much." Noah rubbed Aris's ears. "I had a vision."

Lorcan stiffened. "What did you see?"

"It was a happy one actually. I don't get it, though. I saw a beautiful blue fox, a golden wolf, and a black tiger."

Lorcan rolled his eyes. "The blue fox is me, just so you know."

Noah's jaw dropped. "Wow, really, Uncle Lorcan? It was magnificent!"

"Is there a reason you think I can't be a magnificent blue fox?"

"No, it's so cool. But what about the wolf and the tiger? Who are they?"

"You don't have any question about the fox? Why do you believe me that easily?"

"Because you never tell me lies."

Lorcan nodded. "I think you saw a puma, rather than a black tiger. Before he died, my father said a puma jumped out in front of his car. That was why he veered off the road. I've seen the yellow wolf twice. I'm sure it's some kind of magical creature."

"Werewolf?"

Lorcan nodded. "Are you scared?"

Noah shook his head.

"You said they were friendly in your vision."

"Yes, but I only saw one at a time. I'm not sure if they're friends or not. Was the yellow wolf friendly with you when you saw it?"

Lorcan shook his head. "Not exactly. The problem is I don't know what he wants. I think he might be friendly. He attacked me, but didn't kill me when he had a chance." Lorcan got off the bed, bracing his palms on the wall to keep balance and wishing he'd gotten a bit more rest to regain his energy. He shook his head to chase off his fatigue and went downstairs.

The living room was still the same. The air in the house was still the same. He found his mother in a black dress standing in the middle of the living room. Keeva was bringing her some tea, and Riley trailed just behind her. Everyone turned to look at Lorcan.

He just stood there in the hallway, finding his limbs useless. Jane stood up and approached Lorcan. She embraced him. That felt the same—his mother's embrace. The feel of her body and the sound of her voice, a voice that had soothed his tantrums away when he was just a stubborn kid, were the same.

At this moment, he needed Orla badly. She was the part of his life that he had never taken for granted. He had to fight for her. But his family—or what he had always thought was his family—he had taken it for granted. Now, he had nothing. He had no one.

When he didn't hug his mother back, she looked up at him. He said, "I'm so sorry. I tried to save Father. I tried to pull him back. But the . . ."

Jane put her hand over his mouth to stop him from talking. "None of that was your fault. When you were six, you promised to build me a castle, and you promised to make me proud and happy. I'm still holding you to that."

"You don't hate me? Father died because of me." A tear fell from his eye. Jane wiped it and cupped his face.

"You are my son, my treasure, whether you like it or not. Come sit with me. I want to talk to you, and it will be your decision whether or not you still consider us to be your family."

When everyone had settled around the table in the living room, Jane looked at Lorcan over the rim of her cup of tea.

"We had been just married and were still on our honeymoon. Your father and I went for a picnic at the riverbank, the one he forbade you to go to. We were attacked by wild animals. At least that was the story for the official records. But I knew back then that it wasn't just wild animals."

"Shapeshifters?" Lorcan asked.

Jane nodded. "A whole pack of them. They were going to kill your father, and I couldn't take it. I was on my own in the middle of the woods. I didn't know what to do, so I begged and promised to do whatever it took if they'd spare his life." A tear rolled down her face. "The head of the clan wanted a daughter, and he was going to rape me. I told him I would kill myself if he did, and then he wouldn't have a child with me anyway. I don't know the reason why, but he needed a girl, and he need her within a certain period of time. So I made him a deal."

Lorcan looked at Jane. The tears had dried on her face, but he could see the pain was still raw and fresh.

"I told him if I got pregnant and our first child is a girl, he could have her. I said I would tell no one and lay no claim on the child."

Keeva gasped, and Lorcan saw Riley instantly grab her hand.

Lorcan nodded. He admired Jane—she was a strong woman, and she was fearless when it came to protecting those she loved. "That's how I came along?"

Jane nodded. "I wasn't pregnant at that point. We just had to make sure our first child wasn't a girl. Ferris never told me how he got you. He said it was best if I didn't know. And I always thought it was a closed adoption."

"Then you didn't know about the ten-year limit?"

Jane shook her head. "Not until a few months later. Had I known, I would never have accepted it. But the moment he brought you home, I fell in love with you. You became a part of my life the moment your father brought you through that door. The shapeshifter missed his chance, but he couldn't touch us."

"What stopped him from coming and grabbing Keeva or hurting you and Father if he found out?" Lorcan asked.

"It wasn't just a verbal deal. It was almost like an oath. For magical creatures, that's a big deal. We swore in front of his gods, and they gave me my protection. The lullaby that you always disliked, Lorcan, it would kill anyone in that clan if they broke their promise and tried to harm me or my family."

He remembered now—the lullaby had stopped the monstrous woman at the riverbank from killing him, the woman who had pretended to be Orla and then kissed him and controlled him to upset her. That woman must be from that particular clan of shapeshifters.

"How did you know they attacked me at the riverbank? How did you know to sing the song?"

"It was just gut instinct. I sensed you were coming home. I sensed danger. And the lullaby is the only protection I have for you. My senses when it comes to those shapeshifters are very strong. This time, it felt the same as it did so many years ago, when you came home after you kissed Orla."

"What?"

"Not long before Orla left, you came home reeking with the scent of that shapeshifter clan. You told me you had kissed her for the first time that day. And I knew she was related to them. I knew they were coming for Keeva, but I couldn't tell you why we wouldn't allow you to date Orla."

"But Orla had nothing to do with shapeshifters. Yes, her family does black magic, but it wasn't her choice to be born into that family. She wouldn't have anything to do with the shapeshifter clan you mentioned. Who's the clan's leader?"

"It's Bricius."

There was a buzzing in Lorcan's head. Bricius was one of the most dangerous sorcerers, the one who had cursed his parents and the reason he'd come back to Ireland this time. He was the one he had killed in another dimension.

"Bricius. I've killed him," he muttered.

"But you didn't kill his clan ..." Jane suddenly gasped. "They're coming now!" she said.

Lorcan looked toward the door and saw Alana and a man walking toward them with Maeve trailing behind.

CHAPTER 25

"**W**hich one? Can you tell, Mother?" Lorcan asked.

He recognized Maeve, who had been with Orla before he got shot, and he recognized Alana, who had been holding Orla back when she'd tried to run to him. The two women had seemed to be on Orla's side. But he hadn't seen the man before.

Jane shook her head. "It was just the aura coming from them, but I don't know any of them," Jane said.

Alana walked into the house without invitation and spoke quickly before anyone could say anything. "My name is Alana. This is my cousin Sam. We're from Orla's family. We came to let you know that Orla has agreed to take leadership of our group, and in doing so, she will never see you again. But she did say that you were married in front of God. Therefore, you will have to denounce your marriage in front of our God."

"That's bogus. You guys are holding Orla against her will," Maeve said.

"Shut up, Maeve. You're not part of the family," Alana growled and turned back to Lorcan. "My family will be waiting at the temple at noon tomorrow. If you don't come . . ." She shifted her stance and glanced at Sam for instruction. Sam raised an eyebrow. Alana continued, "If you don't come, Orla will die."

"That's bullshit. It's a trap, Lorcan. They won't bring Orla there," Maeve hissed and pointed her finger at Alana. "Your family never kill their own. So they won't kill Orla."

"That's enough, Maeve," Sam growled.

"You come into my home without invitation, without permission, and you try to lure my son into a trap?" Jane said.

"It's not a trap. The temple is our place of family worship. Orla promised to be with us. All Lorcan has to do is to end their relationship—and do it for her sake. Why would we want to trap him?" Alana said.

"I'm warning you not to go there, Lorcan," Maeve raised her voice.

"It's not your call," Alana snarled.

"Which one of you is from Bricius's clan?" Jane's voice cut through the chaos like a hot knife through butter. She advanced. Lorcan had never seen such animosity in his mother before. "You can all leave except the one from Bricius's clan because that person is responsible for my husband's death."

"Hey!" Alana's voice shook. "We do black magic here!" She pointed her finger at Jane. Lorcan darted forward to stand next to his mother. Keeva and Riley advanced, but he gestured them to stay back.

Alana dropped her finger and withdrew. "We're just the messengers. Lorcan should go to the temple and talk to my family. You can come, too, if you want." Jane moved toward her, and Alana backed away again.

"Let me ask once more, which one of you is from Bricius's clan." Jane's voice was as cold as steel.

Alana turned around. "Sam!"

"What?"

Alana grabbed him and pushed him forward, standing behind him. "Use some of your black magic! She's going to curse us," Alana said to him.

"All right, we've delivered the message. Take it or leave it—it's up to you. We're leaving." Sam turned leave, and Alana scurried after him.

Maeve glared at Jane. "Do you really think pulling a stunt like that is going to work on magical creatures?"

Jane smiled. "I have a very good singing voice. Let me sing you a song and see if you enjoy it. We can talk afterward." Lorcan knew his mother was going to sing the lullaby to see which one reacted to it.

They heard a crash. A large window shattered as a gigantic golden wolf flew through it and head straight at Jane. Lorcan pulled his mother out of the way. The wolf landed on the table, crushing it to pieces.

Alana took one look at the wolf and fainted. Sam cursed and picked her up, rushing outside. The wolf bared its teeth and lunged at Jane. Lorcan shot an electric wave at the wolf. It dropped to the floor in convulsions. Lorcan dropped to his knees, exhausted.

Riley leaped at the wolf and grabbed it. It turned around and bit his right arm then sprung to its feet, running through the door. Lorcan stood up and charged after it, catching up to it at the edge of the woods.

"Hey!" he called out. Lorcan wasn't sure how much energy he had left, but he had a feeling he didn't have anything remaining to shoot at the wolf if it actually attacked him. But the wolf held the answers to many of his questions. He couldn't let it run away again. "Look, I told you before that I'm not going to fight you. I know you want something that I can offer. Let's work it out. I don't think you want to harm us unless we're threatening someone you care for, and that person belongs to Bricius's clan. Am I right?"

The wolf stopped and looked at Lorcan. It quickly glanced back to see if Riley or Keeva had caught up. There was no sign of them. The wolf's lips curled back from its teeth, and a low, rumbling growl came from its throat.

"Right, so we're friends now. Just tell me what you want, and we can work things out. I don't speak wolf, so you'll have to shift back to your human form."

On silent paws, the wolf took a step or two toward Lorcan, then hunkered down low to the ground and lifted its body up into the air in a giant leap, landing squarely on Lorcan's shoulders. The weight of the wolf made Lorcan stumble to the ground. Lorcan scissored his legs and flung the wolf away before it could take a bite of him. He planned to save the last electric shot he had for the worst case scenario.

The wolf and Lorcan circled each other. It wouldn't shift its gaze because it thought he might shoot at it again. But Lorcan wouldn't waste his last beam that easily. The wolf ran out of patience quickly and charged at him again.

Lorcan braced for the impact. He'd learned an Aikido movement when he was younger. When a strong force came at a defender, a circling motion could utilize the force of the attacker. The harder the coming force, the worse the crash. As the wolf landed, Lorcan sidestepped in a half circle, grabbed its neck, swung, and released. The wolf flew through the air and smashed straight into a tree trunk. It howled in pain and crashed to the ground.

Riley and Keeva had arrived. Riley grabbed the wolf and jabbed a needle into it. It wriggled hard, biting and clawing at his arms. Riley held the wolf to the ground, and it whimpered under the pressure.

A wail from somewhere off in the forest made everyone cringe.

CHAPTER 26

It was a howl of pain and outrage, sadness and anger. While Lorcan was busy searching for the source of the sound, the yellow wolf bucked like a wild horse, throwing Riley off and rolling to its feet. Keeva jumped in to help. It took the two of them to force the wolf down again until the tranquilizer took effect.

Lorcan listened to the silence for a few more minutes. He didn't like it and did a mental check of his energy level. One shot was all he had left, he was sure of it. They heard the howl again, but this time it was closer. They heard a loud roar, and then a large shadow landed in front of them. It was a magnificent puma.

Lorcan cursed.

"Stay right here," he said to Riley and Keeva. Then he stood up and ran. The puma leapt after him. He knew he wouldn't be quick enough to outrun it, but he needed to get a bit of distance. The paws of the puma landed on his back. He rolled on the ground and felt blood gushing from his wounds. The puma was growling at him, advancing. He didn't have a good angle to shoot. He stood up and ran again. The animal pounced a second time, catching him in the side with one large paw. Lorcan jammed his foot at the puma's face, pushing it back a bit. He stood and raced off again, stumbling and falling to the ground. Taking advantage of the opportunity, the puma leapt up in the air so that it could land its front paws on Lorcan's chest. While flying, its chest and midsection were open to Lorcan.

He gave it one blast with all he had. The electric current shot out in a wave, curved up, and split into thousands of knives and spears flying at the puma. It roared painfully as the sharp blades hit it. Blood, fur, and flesh rained down to the ground. The puma dropped. It howled and clawed its way into the woods. Lorcan wanted to give chase but he lost sight of the animal as it loped into the cover of the trees.

***

Bradan ran aimlessly through the woods. Maeve had been gone for hours, and he couldn't let her fend for herself out there. They'd never been together, and he knew she would never consider him, but he wanted to tell her how much he cared for her. He couldn't bear the thought that she might never return to him, or that he'd die before he could tell her any of his feelings.

He knew he wasn't talented—in either black or white magic. He was just a guy who had stumbled into a bloodline of magical creatures and was lined up for a position of power. He didn't want it, but he had a responsibility, and people's lives depended on him. He was wrong to tell her he had planned to run away like Orla. The thought had crossed his mind, and he had planned on it—but he was a man. If anything, he had his integrity and honor. He was not going to run away like a little girl.

He had agreed to allow Maeve release the false news that he was dead in order to figure out who the traitor in the clan was and see who surfaced to claim the power. But he had never wanted her to risk her life to do so.

Where is she? he wondered.

He stopped by a tree to catch his breath, and then he saw them. Maeve and Alana, unconscious, bathed in blood. There were body parts scattered on the ground, torn into unrecognizable pieces. Both Maeve and Alana were breathing. He couldn't tell whose blood it was, but it was everywhere.

"Maeve!" He shook her shoulders. No response. He scrambled over to Alana and got the same result. He couldn't take both of them back to the village with him. He could barely walk himself. Bradan pulled them between two large trees and covered them as much as possible with whatever he could find—leaves, weeds, tree branches. Then he charged through the woods for the village.

***

The commotion in the house woke Orla. She wriggled but couldn't free herself from the rope. She was blindfolded. She cursed and struggled even harder. Someone kicked the door in and stormed into the room. She heard Bradan's voice. "Help her, or you won't have either of us." She felt the bed next to her sink down as if someone had lain down there. A burst of light assaulted her eyes when Bradan yanked off her blindfold.

She looked at the person next to her. "Oh God, what happened to Maeve?"

"I don't know. But they won't treat her." Bradan leaned against the wall, a jar in his hand. He was as white as a sheet. At the door, Uncle Tony stood, scowling.

"I don't care for being threatened, Bradan."

"I'm not threatening anyone. You need me or Orla. You care about this jar, so save Maeve."

Bradan removed the rope off Orla.

"Since when did you become completely reckless, Bradan?" Tony snarled.

"That's what we're all about. We do black magic, and we're reckless."

"You're wrong. We aren't reckless. We don't kill our own. And we don't destroy our ancestors' remains. Give me the jar. I will ask Anna to come and look at Maeve."

"I don't believe you. I told you we have a traitor in the clan. They killed my father. I don't know who's who anymore. You want a vessel for your energy at full moon, I'll do it. Just treat Maeve, and let Orla go."

"You're asking for too much, Bradan."

"I'm not asking. I'm telling." Bradan thrust the jar out as if he was going to drop it.

"Okay, calm down, son, I'll call Anna."

Tony backed out of the room. As soon as he'd left, Bradan flopped to the floor.

"Go, Orla. I know you've sworn in just to take that stupid potion for me. But if you don't come at full moon, you should be fine. Now run! As far away as you can."

"You think I'm going to leave Maeve like this?"

"I'll take care of her."

"How can you take care of her? What if she dies?"

"She won't! Maeve wanted to tell Lorcan to get you out of here. She wanted you to be free. If that's what she wanted, I'll do it for her."

"If I leave you, they'll crush you in a heartbeat. And that will break her heart."

"What did you just say?"

"You heard me well enough."

"You . . ."

The door swung open, and Anna stomped in. She scowled at Orla and Maeve and pointed at Bradan. "You. Out. Unless you want to see the girl naked." Bradan scrambled out of the room and slammed the door behind him. Orla knew he stood on guard in front of the door.

CHAPTER 27

Lorcan awoke and found his chest bandaged and his arm in a sling. He shook his head. "You've got to be kidding me, Riley." He got up and pulled his arm out of the sling, put on his wrist unit, and went downstairs.

"You're butchering me!" Riley's voice shot to the hallway from the living room. Lorcan found Keeva cleaning up the gashes on his arms. The wolf had left quite a few bites on Riley even after it had been tranquilized.

"Stay still, Riley. I do this all the time," Keeva said.

"For rabbits and squirrels?" Riley hissed again. Noah sat in a corner rubbing Aris's ears. They both seemed to be enjoying the scene.

"Where's the wolf?" Lorcan asked.

Everyone turned to look at him.

"Apparently you don't need my sling," Riley muttered.

Lorcan chuckled. "But I need your help. Both of you."

Riley shrugged. "Anything except what requires magical talents. We have two in the house, and that's a handful to deal with! Ouch . . . plus the cat . . . plus you . . . Ouch! That's enough, Keeva!"

Keeva let go of his arm while Noah giggled. She stood up from the sofa. "What do you need from me, Lorcan?"

"I'm going to the temple to get Orla out of there. I need you to back me up."

"The woman who came with Orla here before said it's a trap and Orla wouldn't be at the temple."

"That's why I need you. We haven't been married in front of any gods. By telling them that, Orla wants me to walk in there and not have to fight my way in. Once we're together, we can figure a way out. We can't do anything when we're separated from each other."

Riley shook his head. "What a wicked plan!"

Keeva smiled. "I like her already. What about the trap?" Keeva asked.

"There is only one way to find out! But I don't want a fight," Lorcan said.

"I don't see how it's possible without a fight," Riley said.

Keeva glared at him.

"No fighting for any of you," Lorcan said and trailed off when his wrist unit let out a beep. He glanced at it. "Fuck."

"What?" Riley asked.

"There was an accident, and Orla is no longer operating on her natural energy. We didn't have time to set up anything permanent before we came back here. Now her energy is running low. If it runs out, she'll die. I need to get going. Where's the wolf?"

"In the dungeon," Keeva said.

In the old cellar, Lorcan found the wolf chained to a column. His mother stood watching. When the wolf began to shiver, almost like it was cold, Jane took a rag and wrapped it around its body. Lorcan approached, standing next to Jane, and watched. To no one's surprise, the shape of the wolf began to change until it resembled that of a human. A flash of bright light later, and a young man lay upon the floor of the dungeon, still unconscious and clearly naked. Lorcan got up and grabbed some blankets and clothes out of a closet that stood against the stone wall.

Then the man opened his eyes.

"What's your name?" Lorcan asked.

The young man glared at him and looked away.

"All right, I was trying to be polite, but let's cut to the chase. You attacked my mother because she was about to hurt someone you care for. That someone is from Bricius clan. To be honest, I'm no expert when it comes to magic. But I know how to deal."

The man shook his head and smirked.

Lorcan grabbed his neck and shoved him against the wall. "Here is the good news. We've captured them before they got back to the other side of the woods. I'll use one person to trade for Orla. I'll keep one person hostage, and kill one to make my point. Which one of them you *don't* you want me to kill?"

The man glared at Lorcan. He shoved him against the wall one more time.

"Let me offer you something worth considering. I'll let you keep the one you care about, and I'll use the other ones to trade for Orla. However, you have to tell me how to break the curse they put on her. I know with the curse on her, she'll never be free. If you've ever loved someone, you understand what it's like to be tangled up in a curse. You help me out, and I'll help you."

The man contemplated, then he said, "The curse on Orla is based on hatred. It can only be broken by love."

"How?"

"You have to challenge the clan to take your loved one out. They will offer you three choices—a dagger, poison, and a magic strike. If you don't know magic, don't choose that option. I don't know what the poison is, so your safest bet is the dagger."

"The safest?" Lorcan sneered.

"You're a werefox—you can heal quickly. Surely you know how to take a stab and make it nonfatal."

"Hummm. If I break the curse, will Orla be free forever?"

"In theory. *If* that's the only curse she has on her."

"But that means they can put another curse on her, right? And the whole hell cycle will start again?"

"We're were-creatures, not sorcerers . . ."

"There is no *we*. You and I are *very* different kinds, and trust me, you don't want to know what I am. Don't make assumptions. How can I stop them from placing another curse on Orla, or on anyone for that matter?"

"Are you stupid or crazy?"

"Try me!"

CHAPTER 28

The man shook his head, and said, "As an outsider, you can challenge them to a fight to the death to take over their leadership. If you win, you can take the leadership and do whatever you want—including dismissing it. But you know what will happen if you lose."

"What's the challenge?"

"I don't know for certain. But they worship the moon, or its energy. If you destroy the source of their religion, then that should do the trick! Good luck."

"How do you know so much about them?"

The man sneered. "I was in the same boat as you. Didn't have any luck, though. But I've told you all I know. You can go save Orla. Can I have my woman, please?"

Lorcan nodded. "Which one?"

"Alana."

"Alana? The one who fainted at the sight of you?"

The man laughed. "She's a shapeshifter, you idiot. Bricius planted her as a kid in that clan. They trained her to do magic. She can shift in and out of that human form and do magic at the same time. In her true form, she's a hell of a puma. I have to give it to you for capturing her."

"Don't admire me. We didn't get her."

The man's eyes darkened. "What do you mean? You said you had them. I heard her howling before your friend took me out."

"I might have killed the puma. I'm not sure. I was defending myself. But no, I didn't capture her."

"Fuck you, Lorcan. You bastard. You tricked me." The man's eyes reddened, he yanked at the chain.

"Do you know how many people—including women and children—Bricius had killed? And God forbid how many people Alana killed. I can forgive her for trying to kill me at the riverbank, but I won't forgive her clan for what they did to my parents."

"It's not her fault. She was born into Bricius's clan and was chosen as a child. Please don't kill her . . ." Tears rolled down his face. "I've done my best to get her out."

"But did she want out?"

"She couldn't leave. It's her duty. She couldn't get out. Bricius's clan is vicious—you said so yourself. Did you or didn't you kill Alana?" Blood tricked from his nose, and he looked as if his head would explode. He pulled at the chain until it cut into his flesh and made him bleed.

"No. She ran away."

"Let me go. I'll take her away. Please. Just let me go." The man kept tugging at the chain.

"If you couldn't do it before, why can you do it now? If you loved her that much, why didn't you ask your clan to help save her?"

The man roared in anger. More blood trickled from his mouth. "I am a rouge. I have no clan. No master. No home. Alana is all I have. Every time she goes into the woods, she's mine. Let me go!"

"I can't. If she's killing people, I'll have to kill her . . ."

The man roared and then let out a haunting howl. A projectile of blood erupted from his mouth, and then he passed out before he could shift back to his wolf form.

As a pang of guilt stabbed at his chest, Lorcan said, "All right, I'll spare her life if she promises she won't kill anymore . . ." Then he remembered his mother, standing quietly in the corner, listening to the whole conversation without saying a word.

***

Orla scrambled to the bed when Maeve opened her eyes. "Hey, how are you feeling?"

"Where am I?"

Maeve blinked. "You're at Bradan's place. He brought you here."

"Bradan!" Maeve shifted and tried to sit up. Orla pressed Maeve's shoulder to hold her down. "He's fine. It was his decision. He came back and blackmailed Uncle Tony into treating you. I think he's quite cool. I can see now why you love him, Maeve."

Maeve closed her eyes and blushed. Orla cleared her throat. "Thing is, because he's a cool guy, he actually asked me to leave. He said he could take the leadership for me. I can run, you know. But I can't leave you like this, so I stayed. But the point is that Bradan will tell the clan that he's willing the take the leadership, and I can deny it."

Maeve nodded. A tear trickled from her eye and dropped to the pillow.

"What happened in the woods?" Orla asked.

The memory hit Maeve, and she sat straight up. "Oh my God, where are Alana and Sam? Are they okay?"

Orla shook her head. "Bradan found you and Alana unconscious. He found parts of Sam, torn to pieces. Did you see anything in the woods?"

Maeve shook her head. "Everything was a blur. How's Alana?"

"Still out of it."

"I hope she's up and about by the full moon. They'll need a backup for Bradan. If you're not doing it, they'll need her even more."

"To do what?"

"Line up, just in case. She's the next in line after Bradan, but it's just a formality. After the ceremony, she'll go back to London. That's her home. She doesn't belong here."

"Alana is in line for the leadership of the clan?"

Maeve rolled her eyes. "I know. Talking about not wanting to do it, she's the worst of the three of you. I remember Uncle Tony had to drag her kicking and screaming all the way back here. He didn't have any success until her parents died."

Orla narrowed her eyes. "How did they die?"

"Hunting accident."

"Hummm . . ." Her wrist unit beeped, and she glanced at it. "Shit!"

"What's that?"

"I only have fifty percent of my energy left. Long story, but if this thing runs out, I think I'll die."

"Oh my God! How long do you have? What do you have to do?"

"I have no clue. Lorcan knows what to do when it comes to technology. I think I have to go all the way back to our place—very far away from here—with Lorcan to recharge this. I didn't think the energy would run out so quickly. I guess it wouldn't in normal circumstances, but in the last few days, we've been through a lot, haven't we?" She tapped the wrist unit.

CHAPTER 29

The temple was ancient and mysterious. It didn't have to be located in this spooky corner of the woods to emphasize the point, Lorcan thought. He adjusted his wrist unit, making sure everything was in working order. He had already said goodbye to everyone, his plan being to grab Orla and run at any chance he got.

It surprised him that so many people could fit inside the temple courtyard. It wasn't nearly grand as the Egyptian pyramids or Greek temples, but it was quite formidable with stone walls and lofty ceilings.

The double wooden door covered in symbols and letters that he had no clue what they meant. The door slid open as he approached. Lorcan stepped in and noted that the people in the courtyard didn't follow him. He figured that whatever it was he was going to do here was not entertaining enough for spectators.

There was no long aisle with columns or statues leading to a raised platform. It was a simple square room with an altar located right in the center. A large picture of a half moon was displayed prominently in the middle of the altar. The wolf had been right, they worshipped the moon.

His eyes landed on Orla. She was standing next to the altar, smiling at him. Illuminated by candlelight in the mysterious temple, she was beautiful. There were others standing around her. He glanced around, scoping out the number of people, location, and exits.

He heard a low beep and glanced at his wrist unit. But sound hadn't come from his unit, but from Orla's. She didn't look at it, instead keeping her eyes locked with his. He cursed silently. She knew her energy was running low.

An old man stepped forward. "Lorcan, my name is Tony, and I represent the family until the new leader is appointed. You are here to denounce your marriage with Orla Foley."

Lorcan smiled. "Her name is Orla Brody, and until we end our marriage, it will stay that way. I am here to take Orla with me, not to denounce the marriage."

"She owes a great deal to this family. And if I am not mistaken, your life is one of the things she owes us. You can't just walk in here and take her away from us. Who do you think you are?"

"With all due respect, Orla is my wife, and I can't let you force her into a position she doesn't want to take."

"She has sworn."

"Not voluntarily. And where I come from, a promise like that doesn't count."

"I know where you come from. That side of the woods isn't very far from here. But a promise is a promise regardless of where you come from."

Lorcan smiled. "Now that sounds like a threat. She promised to be my wife, and I'm going to hold her to that."

"You are not in a position to judge us . . ." Tony's voice came out so low it was almost a growl.

"I will take the leadership, Uncle Tony. Let Orla go," Bradan spoke up.

"Bradan, you are the second in line. Ideally, we should have Orla."

"Orla has the right to refuse, doesn't she?" Bradan advanced.

Tony narrowed his eyes. "Yes, under normal circumstances, she would have the right to refuse. But she made promises to save his life, and for that she has forfeited all of her rights. Do you want debate the rules with me, Bradan?"

"How can I repay her debts?" Lorcan asked.

"There is no way you can do that, young man. If you denounce your marriage, she stays as leader. If you don't, she will still stay as a magical slave. Either way, she stays and you go."

"There is no point keeping her. I have taken the potion for the ceremony," Bradan said.

"*You* stole the potion?" Tony stared at Bradan in surprise.

"We have a traitor in our clan who killed my father and tried to kill me. I was injured, and without that potion, I would have died."

"Who stole the potion for you?"

"That's irrelevant. I drank it, and the last I heard, Aunt Anna couldn't make a new one in time for the full moon."

"Don't you dare . . ." Tony swung his arm and sent a stream of blue fire at Bradan. Bradan put up his shield just as quickly. The fire was deflected into a column at the corner of the temple, almost breaking it in two.

"You're not the subject today, Bradan. I know you have trained to be the leader, but at the moment, you are not. If you continue behaving in this way, I will not put you in that position."

"You have someone raising his hand for the position. Why insist on Orla?" Lorcan asked.

"You took a wife without honor, Lorcan. You might be married before your God, but you aren't before ours. She didn't have our blessing, and she will spend the rest of her life condemned."

"She doesn't need your blessing, and we don't worship your gods."

Sweat beaded on Orla's forehead. Lorcan knew she didn't have much left in her energy tank. He looked at the old man. If he denounced the marriage to pacify them, they would keep her, and she would die when she ran out of energy. He couldn't tell them about the Daimon Gate and Eudaiz. The multiverse was a secret, and he wasn't going to divulge it. He had to get her out of here, and he had to do it now.

Lorcan advanced. Tony and a line of men standing behind him closed in.

"A fight isn't necessary, Uncle Tony. I promised to take the leadership. Let Orla go," Bradan persisted.

"Do you think she can summon the spirits of our ancestors to save his life in London . . . by herself? I laid the path and connected her. I alone am the guarantor of her oath. She is in my debt. She can't walk away from that."

Bradan sneered, "So that's your true motive, Uncle Tony. I should have known. Because Orla owes you, you will have immediate access to the energy—and a larger share of it when she comes to power. I thought you cared for the clan."

Tony swung his arm, but this time it was too fast for Bradan to put up his shield. He was thrown into the wall like a rag doll and slid down to the floor in a boneless heap. Maeve squealed and crawled out from underneath the altar, scrambling toward Bradan.

"What on Earth is a white witch doing in our temple?" Tony exclaimed and prepared to hit Maeve.

CHAPTER 30

Orla yelled for him to stop. Bradan groggily pulled Maeve behind him to shield her.

"She doesn't belong to this clan. You are not allowed to harm her. So you want to start wars with other clans?" Bradan snarled.

"If you behave as you should, no one will get hurt," Tony growled.

With Tony and the clan distracted, Lorcan seized the opportunity to snatch Orla and make a run for the door.

Tony yelled for them to stop. Before he could swing his arm, Lorcan shot out an electric beam. It scraped the ground in front of Tony, digging a large hole and crumbling all the stone on the floor in the surrounding area.

"I can see you can wield magic, Lorcan. But Orla belongs to us until I release her. You walk through that door, and I will place another curse on her. Her debts will pile up, and she will live her life as a fugitive."

"I don't care, Lorcan," Orla said.

Tony continued, "You might save her now, but her soul will be forever in debt. She has a family, and all she needs is our blessing. She denied us for you, and all you can give her is a life of a thief? Is that how you take a wife in your clan?"

They were at the door, but Lorcan stopped. Orla pulled his arm. "I don't care, Lorcan. As long as we're together, I can live with it. Let's go."

"Don't you dare set foot in Ireland again, Orla. Wherever you run to, consider this home lost to you. You came from dirt, and your parents died for nothing," Tony said in disdain.

Lorcan turned around. "I challenge you and your curses on Orla."

"Lorcan, don't do this," Orla begged.

Lorcan repeated, "I challenge you, Tony, and I challenge your curses and all the magic you've used on Orla. If I win, she will be free to walk out of this clan with no curses and no encumbrances. You will never be able to lay claim on her again."

"How do you know this rule?" Tony narrowed his eyes.

"Are you planning to break the rule, Uncle Tony? This outsider has challenged you. Will you accept or not?" Bradan asked.

"No, Lorcan," Orla cried.

He wiped the tears from her face. "I love you, Orla. If I can't give you the life you deserve, what kind of a husband am I?"

Tony went to the altar and opened a compartment. It didn't surprise Lorcan to see him place a dagger, a bottle of poison, and a piece of dried bone on the table.

"You asked for it. Choose, and I will execute." Tony growled.

"No, Lorcan, no!" Orla cried again. Lorcan looked at Maeve. She nodded and held Orla back.

"I'll take the dagger. And just to confirm, there will be one strike, and if I survive it, Orla will walk free?"

Tony smirked. "Of course."

Lorcan saw the smirk, and he wasn't sure of what to make of it, but if he could take a bullet, he could survive a dagger. But suddenly, he felt a tangible click in his head, and at the back of his eye, a small screen popped up that said, *"Warning. Ten percent survival on execution of the mission."* Then the screen disappeared. Surely his survival chance was higher than that, he thought. Lorcan shook his head to will away his doubt and hesitation.

He stood and looked at Tony. Tony grabbed the dagger and charged at him. He felt a warm glow at his back and saw that Bradan had swiveled to stand right behind him. The force of Tony coming forward was like a raging storm. Lorcan relaxed his shoulders and prepared himself to subtly maneuver his chest so that the dagger wouldn't stab him in the heart.

Then it dawned on him. He could take a strike from a dagger if it was an *ordinary* dagger. But if there was magic involved, he would most certainly be killed. But it was too late now.

As Tony charged and swung the dagger, Bradan placed his palm on Lorcan's back. He felt a wave of warmth, and a shield pulsed forward from inside his body and hung like a curtain in front of him. It was too close for Tony to retract his movement, so he darted through the shield. His body was able to penetrate it naturally because it wasn't designed to block physical forces, but when the dagger hit the shield, particles splattered out of it like liquid and dissolved into the air. Lorcan knew nothing about magic, but he knew that the Bradan's shield had knocked the magic out of the dagger and that Tony planned to use magic on the strike.

The force of the blow pushed Lorcan back a few steps. The impact wasn't as severe as when the bullet had hit him, but he still felt the blow and slumped to the floor, smiling when he realized it had been an ordinary dagger. He saw his blood on the floor, and somewhere in the back of his mind, he heard Orla scream. But at that moment, he knew he had survived the challenge. He felt Orla's arms wrapping around his waist to help him stand up. Her body shook, but her grip was firm.

"I win," he said.

"Uncle Tony, you cheated. He chose the dagger, not the magic, but you combined them. You have disappointed us," Bradan said. "We don't want you as a member of the family anymore. Please leave."

Tony's face looked as if it was on fire, but he said nothing and strode out of the temple.

Lorcan knew he wouldn't be standing for long. He adjusted his wrist unit and opened the portal. In the distance, a flash of light appeared, and the portal opened. Lorcan and Orla could see it, but to the naked eye, it would look appear to be simply a strip of sunlight in the middle of the sky.

The crowd rumbled, "Look at the rainbow! He can create a rainbow in the night sky!"

"Let's go home," Lorcan said to Orla.

Orla helped him as they both walked into the portal, traveling back to Eudaiz.

CHAPTER 31

A beam of bright light assaulted Lorcan's eyes. He squinted and blinked, feeling incredibly groggy. Then he heard Orla's soothing voice and felt her cool hands on his face. The light was too bright. It blinded him, and he blinked again.

"There you are! Hello!" When the light dimmed, he was able to see her smiling face. She kissed his cheek and traced her lips down to his. He stopped the kiss, holding her face up so he could see her eyes.

"Are you okay?"

She grinned. "Perfect." Then she kissed him again.

"Are you okay, Orla? Tell me what's going on, honey." Then he saw a bracelet strapped to his right wrist, one similar to Orla's. "Crap." He winced and sat up. He was lying on a lab bench and wearing something that looked like a hospital gown. "What the hell is this?" He pulled at the gown that was a definite insult to his fashion sense.

"Orla, where are we?"

"Eudaiz."

"Oh, so we made it?"

"Not exactly. Ciaran got us half way."

He shrugged. "That's all right. He can brag for the rest of his life that I never complete a mission without his help."

Orla took a set of clothes over to him, and Lorcan slid into his jeans. Before he pulled his shirt on, he noticed that the dagger had left a large red scar on his chest. That surprised him because the injuries he'd suffered before hadn't left any trace after he'd healed himself, and they'd been, in his opinion, much more severe than this stab wound.

"Ciaran said your defense system, the one that helps you heal impossible injuries, was very low—or in his words, non-existent—when you took the dagger."

Lorcan nodded. "All right, I might have miscalculated a little bit . . ."

"Miscalculated?" Tears gleamed in Orla's eyes. "You knew your chance of survival was less than ten percent. You didn't calculate at all, but your artificial brain did. That robot warned you!" She jabbed her finger into his chest, tears rolling down her face.

He remembered the little screen that had flipped on in the back of his eyes, warning him of the danger. "How did you know that?"

"We almost didn't make it. My energy was running out. You couldn't walk anymore. I was sure that we would be dead halfway into the transitional zone. And then, Ciaran came to rescue us." More tears rolled down her face now.

He wiped the tears and kissed her cheek.

"And then you didn't wake up as you had before. The wound wouldn't heal. Ciaran said you were in trouble, so he brought you to this lab."

Orla walked over to the window and looked outside. Lorcan embraced her from behind and found her body shaking with emotion. She turned around and looked him in the eye. "Ciaran did an entire profile analysis of you. I don't know how he did it. You can ask him for the details."

"I only care about the details that draw tears out of your eyes."

She gazed at him for a long moment in silence. Then she sighed. "You are programmed to love me."

He released her from his embrace. "You think I'm a robot? You think my feelings for you have no emotional grounds?"

"I don't *think*, Lorcan. It's a fact." She waved her arms in the air. "Fifty percent of you was artificially created. Your brain was wired to tell you would fall in love with the first girl who made your heart skip a beat. That explains everything."

"What does it explain?"

"Why you always followed me. Why you loved me regardless of how I treated you. Why you loved me for no apparent reason. It explains the childhood sweetheart story. What you've got with me, you could have had with any girl, Lorcan. But why me? Because you were *wired* to love me."

218

The emotion coming out of her was like a horrific storm, and it stabbed at his heart. The pain was incredible.

"But what about my human half? My parents thought you were related to Bricius. They told me if I chose to leave home to look for you in London, they'd never want to see me again. But I chose you over those I thought were my family. Emotions can't be programmed! You can program a robot to do anything, but you can't program it to love. You can't program a robot to compare, prioritize, and choose between family relationships and romantic love!" He paced the room as he spoke, wanting to smash something. "Now that I've turned out to be a thing and not a person, my feelings mean nothing to you? Our lives together, our stories, what we have done together . . . you disregard everything because I'm not human?"

"No, it's not that . . ."

"It's not *that*? So what the fuck is it? What did I do with my fucking life—making fucking stupid decisions, giving up my family, and oh, hang on, that doesn't matter because they're not even my fucking family! I don't need a fucking family. Why? Because I'm arti-fuckingly created."

"The profanity is unnecessary, Lorcan."

He waved his arms in the air. "Sorry! There's nothing I can do about it because it was fucking wired in my brain that way!"

The tears in her eyes had dried. She simply looked at him and waited until he finished his rant. Then she sighed. "I'm sorry, Lorcan. It was just one of my weak moments."

"You don't have weak moments, Orla. You kicked me around like a soccer ball for years." He went to the window and looked outside. He noted that the garden outside the lab was artificial—the lawn, the flowers, the trees, and maybe even the air as well. The garden looked perfect, but he was far from being perfect. He was defective. He turned and looked at Orla, and he would have rather seen tears than what he saw on her face.

He had hurt her.

He wished she would yell at him, call him names. But she didn't. "Lorcan, I was just wondering if you would ever choose me if your attraction to me were natural? Before all of this, there were countless times I asked myself if your love for me was real. But I love you. I've given you all I've got. It hurt too much for me to contemplate the slightest chance that you didn't love me back. So I just pretended I didn't question anything."

He didn't have an answer—for her or for himself. The pain stabbed at his heart, at his brain. He wondered if that was artificial, too. Surely pain couldn't be programmed. He didn't ever want to cause Orla pain. He wanted her to know his love was natural, and he wanted to know that for himself as well.

Maybe there was only one way to find out.

CHAPTER 32

Lorcan's knees buckled. He slumped to the floor. He felt Orla's grip, and then he felt nothing else. But he could still hear her. He heard Ciaran's voice, too. He was glad nobody asked him anything because he couldn't seem to speak.

"The wound healed. Why is it bleeding now?" Orla asked.

"His body is too weak to handle the injury naturally. He's relying on other parts to help him survive until he can naturally gain some strength back. His body is rejecting the supernatural part. If he totally disengages with it, he'll die," Ciaran said.

"What are you talking about?"

"Orla, the supernatural part of him is like an implant. His body accepted it well before. I don't know why he's rejecting it now. What did you say to him?"

"I just asked him if he would naturally love me, even if he wasn't programmed to."

"Jesus Christ, Orla! The human brain drives emotions. It can't be programmed. Love is not in DNA—it's in the heart and soul. You guys are soulmates, and if you can't see that, there's nothing I can do to help you—or him."

"It's my fault . . ." Orla cried.

"Beat yourself up later. Grab that machine. I need to resuscitate him. He's shutting his robotic part down."

"No."

"What? If he doesn't reconnect with that part of him, he'll die."

"Will resuscitation connect the two parts?"

"No. But I'm running out of options here!"

"Let me talk to him."

"Orla!"

"Let me talk to him. Please."

And then he heard her voice whispering in his ear, "Lorcan, I love you. If you want to love me back, you have to stay alive. I need you to borrow some of the supernatural power. I know I've made you hate it. But please try . . . for me . . ."

He wanted to try, but he was just so goddam tired. Maybe he just needed to sleep. He blocked her voice out and drifted to a dark and quiet place for some peaceful rest. But suddenly it was like lying on a train track when the train was near. He felt his shoulders shaking, and he heard Orla's voice again. She was saying something, crying maybe. Maybe if he tried a little harder, she'd let him sleep.

He didn't know how much time had passed.

A beam of bright light assaulted his eyes again. He squinted, blinked. Then he heard Orla's soothing voice and felt her cool hands on his face. "Here you are! Hello again!" When the light dimmed, he was greeted by her smiling face.

"How long was I out?"

"Too long. And before you ask, let me say this . . . I love you too much to lose you again. I know you come with extras, like the supernatural part of you and all the cool tricks it can do. So if you ever try to disconnect from your superpower again, I will go back to my clan and figure out a curse to hunt you down regardless of where you may be in this multiverse."

"Now I'm scared. Can I sit up?"

"Sure."

Before he hopped up, she planted a kiss on his lips and pressed him back down again. Her hands were busy on his body, and his breath caught so damn quickly. He could feel his body vibrating uncontrollably.

"Are we on a lab bench?" he asked while his hands pulled at her clothes as if he was possessed.

"Yes, and I think this session is being recorded."

"Anything for research." He flipped her over so that she lay on her back, and then he ravished her.

***

Later, Orla was curled into his side, sleeping. The lab door opened, and they scrambled to their feet. Ciaran walked in. "I see you're up and well." He sat down opposite the two of them. "You've got quite the supernatural makeup, Lorcan."

"What kind of creature am I exactly?"

Ciaran laughed. "Yes, for lack of vocabulary, I think we can settle on *creature*. Your human DNA comes from your father. You knew that part. But your emotional and psychological profile comes from your mother. And that fascinates me because you're the perfect combination of nature and nurture."

Lorcan scowled. "I'm not your lab rat."

"Certainly not. But you're sombody's, and I happen to know the person who created you and what she tried to accomplish."

"When will you give me that information?"

"I can't tell you about your maker, but I can let you know everything about yourself . . . when you're ready."

Lorcan nodded and raked his hands through his hair. "We have to go back to Ireland to finish our business there. Then I'll be ready. How long has it been since we left?"

Ciaran stood. "A couple of days at the most. Do you need my help this time?"

Lorcan nodded. "Not you personally, but we'll definitely need people."

Ciaran smiled. "I'll see what I can do."

CHAPTER 33

Tonight was the night. Orla gazed at the altar in the temple from a distance. The doors of the temple were open, and a large group of people gathered outside. In front of the altar, Bradan stood in his ceremonial robe. The senior members of the family flanked his sides. They were waiting for the magical moment.

Outside the temple was a raised platform, set up so that the new leader could receive the energy from the moon.

There was no sign of Maeve. Orla knew her friend wouldn't be anywhere near this place during this moment. She would be crying her eyes out somewhere in the woods. She felt a tug at her arms and felt Lorcan's warm hands holding her.

"We will stop all of the suffering. Do you trust me?" he asked.

"I do."

They heard the chanting sound of praying from the temple and saw that the moon had come into position. Bradan left the temple and went outside. He walked to the raised platform and looked up to the moon. He was quite a formidable character and would make a good leader if not for the dark magic, Orla thought.

Among the senior people in the family, Alana stood solemnly.

"There she is," Orla pointed.

Lorcan nodded. "What do you think she'll do?"

"I'm not sure yet. None of them know she's a traitor and a shapeshifter. I can't see how she could take the leadership naturally while Bradan is alive. After he absorbs the energy from the moon, there will be nothing anyone can do to remove it."

"Can she use black magic to kill him?"

"No. There are so many senior people around, she'd get caught. Plus he could shield himself from the energy and magic."

The crowd had finished their praying and started to cheer as the magical moment crept closer.

"She signaled. Did you see that?" Orla asked.

"Yes," Lorcan responded as Alana twirled her hair and angled the ring she was wearing to the sky. He saw it let out a faint spark. Lorcan adjusted his wrist unit to signal his people.

Bradan winced and touched the back of his neck.

"They shot him," Orla said and jumped out of their hiding place.

Lorcan pulled her back. "We have to wait, Orla. Don't ruin the plan."

On the raised platform, Bradan swayed and slumped to his knees. The crowd gasped and grumbled in confusion. Aunt Anna rushed to Bradan. A stream of dark blood trickled down his nose.

"He's poisoned," Orla said. "I have to help him."

"How?" Lorcan asked.

"I don't know."

From the chaotic crowd, Maeve jumped onto the raised platform and grabbed for Bradan who was turning bluer by the second. Blood started to come out of his mouth. He tried to say something to her, but all that came out was blood. She pulled out her potion and tilted it into his mouth.

The crowd protested.

"White witch, what's she doing here?"

"White witch, get out of here!"

Maeve ignored the crowd. Bradan coughed out some red blood and leaned into her arms. She helped him up. The crowd yelled for Maeve to get off the platform.

"He needs treatment, or he'll die," Maeve explained.

"Let them go," Anna said.

The crowd quieted down and split in half, leaving a path for Maeve and Bradan. She shifted, taking most of Bradan's weight, and walked down the path. Someone in the crowd objected, yelling and insulting Maeve, but no one touched them. Maeve and Bradan struggled through the crowd, heading toward the woods.

"I have to help them," Orla said.

"I'll wait here. Be very careful, Orla. In case we get separated, I'll open the portal at the riverbank.

Promise me you'll make it there." Lorcan grabbed Orla's hand.

"Yes. Promise me you will be there, too."

He nodded. She kissed him and headed in the direction of Maeve and Bradan.

***

The crowd grew noisier as Bradan and Maeve disappeared into the woods. Aunt Anna stood on the platform, glancing around. Alana smiled to herself. She had worked her whole life and sacrificed everything she for this moment. Her clan should be proud of her. She glanced up to the platform and met Anna's eyes.

"Alana," Anna called out.

Alana smiled openly. "Yes."

"You are the third in line. Step forward."

Alana wished she could tell Anna how much she hated the look on her face, her magic, her medicine, and everything else about her. The minute she became the leader of this family, Anna's garden would be the first to go. It would give Alana so much pleasure to see Anna suffer. Anna looked at her with disdain and said, "Kneel. Swear to our Gods right here. No need to go inside the temple."

Of course she would do it right here. She kneeled and swore to the Gods of this family. She would do whatever it took to take this clan over, and then to wipe it out and grind it into dust to make them all pay for her pain. Her whole life had been leading up to this moment. *Swear in, become the leader, take the power from the Gods*, Alana thought. Then she would release the bad news with pleasure - the power would not be distributed to their clan but to her shapeshifter family. She would enjoy that moment much more than this ceremony.

Bricius had to be proud of her, wherever he was.

Alana wanted to laugh out loud. She hated this clan so much she could eat them alive right now.

"Alana!" Anna scolded.

"Yes."

"Are you done?"

Yes, of course." She stood and looked up to the moon. It was almost time.

CHAPTER 34

Bradan fell to the ground, exhausted. "Leave me here, Maeve. Go back to the ceremony. Whoever wanted me dead is causing trouble there. Alana is third in line, but I'm not sure she is up to the task."

"Wake up, Bradan. They treated us like that, and you still worry about them? I wonder sometimes how on earth you belong to that black magic clan. Keep going. I don't want to be dinner for the shapeshifters."

"Too late, it seems," Bradan said. With strength he had left, he lifted Maeve up, and she grabbed a tree branch and hopped up onto it. They heard the movements of several animals accompanied by deep growls. Maeve reached down to help Bradan climb up, but he didn't take her hand. Instead, he drew out a pair of hunting knives.

Three leopards leaped out from the bush. Maeve had to admit that Bradan was quick as lightning. Although weakened by the poison and knowing no magic, his combat skills were more than respectable. With a few moves, he took down two animals. The third one tore up his shoulder before he killed it.

Maeve jumped back to the ground. Before they could move, there was the sound of animals moving in a herd. "Holy crap." Bradan shook his head. He turned around, wanting to lift Maeve up into the tree again, but she backed away. "There's no way you can take down this many. I'll stay with you."

Before Bradan could protest, they saw the reflection of wild animal eyes scattered among the trees. They advanced on the two of them. Bradan pushed Maeve against a tree trunk behind him. He turned to a press a deep kiss onto her lips. Then he gripped his knives.

The animals came.

From behind them, Orla charged forward, hands curled into fists and fireballs flying at the animals. They howled in pain and burned like torches. In a short moment, the woods returned to its quietness. Orla turned around to see Maeve and Bradan gaping at her. She shrugged, "I've done this before. Once or twice."

She looked again at a dark corner of the woods. "Crap. They're heading toward Lorcan's home."

Orla stood at and looked in the direction of the ceremony, the opposite direction to his home. She looked at her wrist unit but had no idea how to operate it.

"Hell!" She rushed off toward Lorcan's home. Maeve and Bradan followed her. "What are you doing? You can hardly walk! You'll slow me down, Bradan," Orla said.

"You'll need my shield," he said and let Maeve help him run after Orla.

***

Lorcan glanced around. What was taking Orla so long? He might have to finish this himself. Alana had sworn in and was proceeding to receiving her leadership. The next step would be receiving the power from the moon. It was critical they intercept her after she had sworn in—but before she received the full moon's energy.

Alana stood on the platform and was proceeding toward the last step. Lorcan had no choice but to execute the plan. He came out from his hiding place.

"Stop!" he said.

On the platform, Alana turned at look at him. Her expression was priceless.

"What?" It was a growl loaded with tons of explosive fury from Alana.

"I can see that you are the new leader of this clan, and I am here to challenge this clan and your leadership."

"You want to do *what?*" Alana roared.

"I challenge your leadership," Lorcan repeated.

"You wouldn't dare!" Alana whirled, her eyes bloodshot and beads of sweat running down her forehead. She adjusted her stance, and her eyes went blank. Lorcan knew black magic was coming his way. He concentrated and shot an electric wave at the platform right in front of Alana. It dug a large hole and cracked the surface. The crowd withdrew.

Alana jumped down to the ground.

"Now we're on a level playing field." Lorcan smiled. "You look like you'd like to use magic on me. That's not an appropriate response to an outsider's challenge of the leadership. If you are too new to the position to know, this is your second chance to respond properly."

Alana smirked. "Do you know what will happen if you lose?"

"I don't plan to lose, but yes, I know the consequences."

Alana smiled. "All right. To win this challenge, you have to burn our energy source . . ."

"I do indeed." Lorcan looked at the crowd, which had backed several feet away. Even the senior clan members stood at a distance.

Alana and Lorcan circled, looking at each other like predator and prey. Lorcan smiled. He glanced at the crowd and then concentrated. He turned his face up to the moon, gazed at it, and shot a large wave of electric current into the air. He used so much energy that it sent him staggering backward.

A funnel of smoke appeared, twirled, and flew straight at the moon. He heard a clashing sound, and the image of the moon cracked and shook.

There were sparks, and each spark of purple light sent the crowd staggering back further. Lightning stretched across the sky, straight to the moon. Explosion after explosion burst blood red in the dark sky.

The moon caught on fire. The round shape of the moon became redder by the second. The heat of the fire burned the trees around them. They could smell the smoke and feel the heat. People in the crowd cried out, tears in their eyes. They slumped to their knees and started praying.

Lorcan cast a dismissive glance at Alana, who looked as if he would set him on fire if she could.

The moon still glowed red. Lorcan had burned the moon, the source of the clan's energy.

"You tricked me. You must be cheating. This isn't possible," Alana roared.

The entire clan was on their knees.

"They don't think I'm cheating." Lorcan gestured at the crowd.

"Liar. You have to be." Alana advanced and raised her arms, ready to perform magic. Lorcan shot another electric wave at her. She jumped and rolled on the ground to avoid it.

All senior members of the clan approached Lorcan. Anna stepped forward. "You have won the leadership challenge. What would you like to do?"

"I want Alana out of the clan. I want Maeve to be leader. If she doesn't accept, then I want Bradan. All rules of the clan that restrict positive emotions and relationship are to be abolished. New rules will be formed, and it will be up to the new leader—either Bradan or Maeve."

"No!" Alana roared and charged at Lorcan. Anna swung her arm, and a stream of fire shot at Alana. Alana twirled to avoid the burst of fire. Her body stretched out, and she grew to twenty feet, her arms becoming gigantic claws. Lorcan looked up and wasn't surprised at all to see a hideous version of the woman at the riverbank. Her long, sharp claws stretched out like iron snakes. They pierced Anna and lifted her off the ground. Blood rained down on the people as Alana laughed. People trampled each other, running to get away.

"This is the price for stopping me from getting what I want. Do you like this, Lorcan?"

"Give up, Alana. You've lost," Lorcan said.

"Over my dead body. I am the leader of this clan. It is mine!" Alana screamed and shot fire at Lorcan.

The force lifted him up and threw him into a tree. From the corner of his eyes, he saw Riley running toward him. Lorcan smiled and glanced up at Alana.

"This is your last chance, Alana. Give up your leadership. Go away."

***

Orla ran as fast as she could. The air vibrated with the energy of the coming shapeshifter. Maeve and Bradan trailed right behind. Orla worked her head frantically, searching for the information Ciaran had gathered about Lorcan and his parents. Why were they attacking Lorcan's home? If Alana was the key to their plan, and she was to get them the power, what would attacking Lorcan's home give them?

She kept running.

When she got a glimpse of a small group of shapeshifters, she charged straight at them and let her fireballs fly. She took them down quickly—too quickly for her liking. She was missing something.

She kept running toward Lorcan's home. She could see the entrance from the distance. She skidded to a halt, and Maeve slammed straight into her.

"Holy crap," Orla said.

The leopard shapeshifters had surrounded the house. There was no way she could take all of them down. The people in the house, aware of the attack, had turned the lights off, but that would put them at a disadvantage. Darkness was what these animals were used to.

Lorcan had said Alana was from Bricius's clan, and the wolf he'd captured was her lover. How much she loved the wolf, Orla had no clue. But she might send other leopards here to rescue it. There were problems with her theory. First, the number of leopards present here was definitely overkill for rescuing a single wolf from a group of defenseless women and children. And second, Alana didn't know Lorcan had the wolf and was keeping it here.

Then something dawned on her. Lorcan's father had been on his way to give Lorcan information about his origin when a leopard caused the accident that had cost him his life. That meant the leopard—or Bricius's clan—knew about Lorcan. They knew he was not their biological son, and therefore knew that Keeva was their first child. Jane had promised their first child to Bricius if the child was a girl.

It was obvious to Orla that the leopards weren't trying to rescue the wolf. They were going for Keeva.

CHAPTER 35

Lying on the ground, looking up at the demonic version of Alana, Lorcan said, "Give up your leadership pursuit, Alana. I know you've worked your whole life for this, but it's over. I want to spare your life."

Alana laughed. "How kind of you, thinking about sparing my life while I am kicking your ass!" She laughed again, but the laugh grew bitter.

Lorcan saw a broken soul beneath the evil facade. At the riverbank, he knew she had meant some of what she'd said. She'd used magic to read his mind and had stumbled upon the memories of him stalking Orla during his childhood. She'd tapped into it, and it had chewed up her subconscious and had become her own memories. When she'd said she wanted a taste of him, what she had meant was she'd wanted a taste of true love—and not with him but with someone special in her life.

Alana didn't have many choices. Lorcan pitied her. "You're outnumbered, Alana. Let this go and live," he said.

"Do you think I'm stupid enough to fight this whole clan by myself?" She snapped her fingers, and herds of pumas and leopards emerged from the depths of the darkness, stealthily walking around and closing everyone in. "This is my true family," she said. "I'll let this clan live, but they will live the way I want them to. As for you, Lorcan, you destroyed the source of energy I've worked for years to get. I can't forgive you for that."

Lorcan stood up slowly and glared at the animals.

"Sorry, Lorcan," Alana said and signaled.

Two pumas jumped at him. He stepped back, fixed his stance, and shot a large electronic wave at them. They howled, dropped to the ground, and disintegrated.

Alana smiled and raised her arms. She was ready to call the group of them to attack Lorcan.

But just then they heard a loud, haunting howl. The shadow of a warrior and an army of wolves appeared.

Lorcan smiled. They had made it in time. It was his friend, Roy, a half-wolf, half-fox were-creature. Obviously, Ciaran had given him an army of creatures to lead. And they weren't ordinary werewolves - they were super powerful space were-creatures.

The shapeshifter leopards and pumas cringed and shrunk into disorganized small groups. The space creatures were double their size.

Alana glanced at her surrendering clan. "You cowards! Fight! Don't just stand there!"

From behind the line of space creatures, Roy stepped forward and approached Lorcan. "Sorry I'm late," he said. "We had a change of plans." Lorcan looked behind Roy and couldn't find Mori. "The shapeshifters split," explained Roy. "Half of them attacked your home. So we split as well. Mori is heading toward your home to handle that half," Roy whispered into Lorcan's ear.

The hair at the back of his neck stood up, and a surge of fear stabbed at this heart. Attacking his home? With this mother, sister, Noah, and a kitten inside? How could he have made such mistake? Why hadn't he thought of that?

"How many?" Lorcan asked.

"Don't know. We split half of what we've got."

"Did you see Orla?"

Roy shook his head. Riley arrived, holding a bag in one hand and a rifle in the other. "It was harder than I thought, but we've got it."

Lorcan felt sweat running down his spine. He had to finish the business here quickly, find Orla, and get back home.

"As I said, Alana, you're outnumbered. I've given you a chance to withdraw, and you didn't take it. So I guess you'd rather die," Lorcan said.

A corner of Alana's mouth quirked up. "Intriguing. I am the best of the shapeshifters. Even if I don't take this leadership, killing me isn't possible for you."

"You have no clan, no group, and no master now. I'm guessing you'd like to be a rogue. So go with your friend. You can be together in hell."

Lorcan tossed out the contents of the bag Riley had given him. On the ground lay the golden wolf skin, the fur soaked with blood.

"Your friend wouldn't give up your location or your identity. He died protecting you, Alana." He could see the blood surging beneath her skin. "The reason I gave you a second chance was because beneath that mask, I know you are a woman who could love. Or should I say, a woman who used to love. The wolf told me all about the time you spent in the woods with him."

Alana roared and grew larger. Then she shrunk considerably and fell to the ground.

"He said you left him for power, and he would rather die than live without you. When he found you, he didn't want to be a rouge anymore. He thought he had found his other half. A life partner."

Alana opened her mouth to say something but it came out as a guttural animal growl. Lorcan's plan might work. If she'd had a fraction of true love for the wolf and had sworn in to this black magic clan, the conflicting emotions would kill her. She would burst into flames at any second. That was, if she had ever loved the wolf.

Lorcan continued, "Before I ripped his skin apart from his body, he was telling me about the time the two of you had run together in the woods. He treasured that and said he would do whatever it took to free you from your duty to your clan. But you loved power too much. And that broke his heart."

Alana roared one more time. Riley aimed his rifle. Roy pulled his gun.

She leaped toward Lorcan and then dropped to the ground. Then she stretched her arms out, and for a moment, her hands turned into the gigantic paws of a black puma. The black magic clan roared in anger. They yelled and cursed and wanted to trample her to death.

Lorcan stopped the crowd. "She'll die soon by herself because of her own curse and her betrayal to her true love."

She couldn't shift. The paws turned back into human hands, and she turned back into a beautiful and dying Alana. She lay on the ground, tears pouring from eyes that had begun to burn with fire.

She didn't beg. She didn't talk. She just waited for her death.

Lorcan crouched next to her. "Why did you send your clan to my home?"

"I didn't. They found out about your make. Now they want Keeva. I am not that important to them. I'm just a pawn."

His heart skipped several beats. His little sister was what they wanted. Lorcan turned to Riley who had no idea what was going on back at home. Lorcan could feel the heat seeping out from every pore in Alana's body. She was going to burst into flames.

They still had the wolf locked up—the fur had just been a decoy.

"I won the challenge. Is there anything I can do to help you?" Lorcan asked.

Tears rolled down her face. "Did he really think I left him for power?"

Lorcan couldn't lie to the dying woman. "No. He loves you."

Alana nodded. "Thank you." And she closed her eyes.

They heard a low growl and saw a shadow fly out from the woods. The yellow wolf leapt out in one swift move, flipped Alana onto its back, and charged into the woods. People roared and wanted to give chase, but Lorcan stopped them.

"Let them go. Your clan isn't exactly saintly. So for all the sins you've committed and the people you've killed or harmed with your black magic, let this even out the game. Let's forget and move on," Lorcan said to the crowd.

He turned toward Riley and Roy. "Shapeshifters attacked my home. The wolf is here, so I don't know what's happening at home or why they released it." Then he ran in the direction of his home. Riley and Roy followed.

The run home through the woods seemed to take forever.

CHAPTER 36

In the house, Keeva grabbed the rifle and walked toward the door. Jane banged at the door of her room and shouted for Keeva. "Keeva, let me out. I won't tolerate this."

"She's really mad, Keeva," Noah said. The kitten, Aris, sat on his shoulder, giving Keeva a disapproving look.

"Now, for you two, I'll lock you in your room, too." Keeva picked Noah up. Noah wriggled and protested.

"I can do magic, Keeva. Orla taught me. I can help."

"I can't let a kid fight."

251

"Let me down. You just wait here. Father will be back. He always keeps his promises. If I let you go out there and you get hurt, he'll be mad."

"Stop wriggling. I'll wait if I can. I thought we had a wolf to use to bargain with the shapeshifters. They lurked around for hours and didn't attack because we had the wolf. It's one of them. But Mother let it go, and now we've got nothing, Noah. Do you understand that? They will storm in here shortly, and I need to put you somewhere safe."

"But how many can you kill with that rifle?"

"I don't know, but I won't go down that easily."

"No one is going down. Let me go. I had a happy vision, and if you stay alive, it will happen."

Keeva put Noah down. "What was your happy vision?"

"You and Father, me and Aris were having a picnic at the riverbank."

Keeva looked into Noah eyes. "That's a happy thought. But no one is having picnic at the riverbank in the middle of winter. You're making this up, aren't you?" Keeva tilted Noah's chin up and looked into his eyes. Noah pouted and tears threatened.

"You promised my mother!"

"I didn't promise anyone anything!"

"You promised you'd take care of me and Father. Please—just stay in here and wait."

They heard a crash. The side window broke, and a gigantic shadow leapt in, landing smoothly and quietly on the floor. Keeva raised the rifle, aiming at the creature. In front of them was a magnificent leopard with glowing green eyes. Keeva held the rifle firmly. "I never harm animals, but I'll make an exception this time. You're not just an animal, and I have a kid to protect."

The leopard whirled around stealthily, then its fur glowed for a second before it turned into a man—tall, lean, and young with striking green eyes.

"There you are. You weren't hard to find at all. What a magnificent creature! Now I understand why he wanted you so much." He looked Keeva up and down.

"Who?"

"Our late leader. But don't worry, we'll treat you well."

"Thank you very much. But I'm the one with the gun, and I am *not* in the mood to treat any one well at the moment. What do you want?"

"You, of course," the man nodded at Keeva.

"Well, you are not going to get me. Aside from me shooting you, what can I do to get you out of my home?"

In the blink of an eye, the man shifted back into leopard form and leapt at Keeva.

Without hesitation, she pulled the trigger.

CHAPTER 37

The sound of the bullet terrified the wild animals in the woods as much as the shapeshifters around the house. The shapeshifters closed in, howling, barking, and roaring to intimidate.

From behind the shapeshifter lines, Orla, Maeve, and Bradan rushed in. Orla threw fireballs at them, nonstop, one after another. As the ones in the back howled in pain and burned like torches, the front line turned around. They ran in circles to surround Orla, Maeve, and Bradan.

From this end of the woods, the moon was full, bright yellow and clear, shedding enough light for Orla to see that they were outnumbered by the were-creatures. She kept hurling her fireballs, but she wasn't sure how long they could hold on. They stood, their backs toward one another, while the animals ran circles around them. The animals closed the circles, tighter by the minute. They were so close she could hear them breathe.

"Behind me," Orla said. Bradan and Maeve could fight with magic, but when the animals commenced a physical attack, there was nothing much they could do except engaging in hand-to-hand combat. Orla threw more fireballs to the front of her. At the back, Maeve and Bradan fought some shapeshifters off when they got close.

Orla turned to throw a couple of fireballs and heard a growl at her back. A puma's paw slapped at her shoulder, throwing her a few feet away. She scrambled to her feet and tossed more balls of fire in the directions of her attackers. Maeve and Bradan stood back to back. They wouldn't be able to hang on for long.

The door of the house opened, and Keeva yelled, "In here!" Orla, Maeve, and Bradan raced inside.

Before Keeva could close the door, a smaller puma leapt toward it. It was too fast for Keeva to use her rifle. Orla was running in and didn't see it.

They saw a small fireball the size of a tennis ball hit the puma right between the eyes. He howled and ran away. Keeva slammed the door closed and saw Noah behind her, hands still curled into fists. "The fire was small, but it did the job," Noah said when Keeva glared at him.

Keeva pointed to the broken window. "The others are secured with thick wooden doors. That's the only window broken." They guarded the one window, hitting any shapeshifters that attempted to enter with a fireball or a bullet. The animals seemed to understand the risks. Eventually, none tried to invade through that window.

Orla saw the leopard, now a man, tied to a chair. "He thought I wouldn't shoot him, so I got him in the leg," Keeva said.

"You're a hell of a shot, Keeva. Ask Lorcan to shoot at an elephant at two feet, he'll still miss, I guarantee," Orla said.

Keeva laughed. "I'm glad there's something I can do better than him. Now that he's turning supernatural and all that, he'll be unbearable."

"No one can compete with you in being his sister, Keeva. You and your mother are the two most important women in Lorcan's world. Trust me."

"What about you?"

Orla merely smiled and said nothing. Lorcan and she were soulmates. There was no need for reassurance.

"Your shoulder is soaked in blood, Orla," Maeve said. Orla looked at her injury, realizing she couldn't heal as fast as Lorcan did. "I'm okay. Where's Jane?" Orla asked Keeva.

"She released the wolf. Keeva got mad and locked her in her room," Noah said.

"Thank you, Noah! I guess I'm not able to speak for myself," Keeva said and pinched Noah's nose lightly.

Orla peeked through the window and looked outside. The shapeshifters were lurking around, waiting for an opportunity to attack. "Bradan and Maeve, could you watch the window?"

"Sure," Bradan said.

"I need to talk to Jane. Can you keep an eye on Noah?" Orla asked Keeva. Keeva nodded. "Mother is in the room at the end of the corridor on the left."

Orla went to Jane's room. She knocked and removed the chair Keeva had used to jam the door from the outside. Orla entered and found Jane sitting at the side of her bed. It wasn't just a room, it was a grand master suite. The room was elegantly decorated and there wasn't a single wrinkle on the bed linens. Not a single thing out of place.

From years working as a high-end antique thief, Orla knew exactly how women in upper class families behaved, reacted, and dealt with life. She knew how they handled pain, loss, happiness, family, lifestyle and—in rare instances—maintained their sanity. The room in front of her was an example of how much pain this woman had suffered and how much control she had.

Jane was a role model for controlling emotions.

Jane stood when she saw Orla. Her movements were gracious, but Orla knew there was a storm of turmoil inside her. Not exactly the ideal situation to be introduced to a mother-in-law. She cleared her throat and spoke, "I'm Orla . . ."

Jane smiled. "I know. I've seen your pictures."

Orla nodded. "I shouldn't be so naive as to think that you didn't keep tabs on Lorcan's life."

"Not as much as I would have liked to."

"The shapeshifters are surrounding us. I think we should get everyone out of here. If they decide to attack us all at once, we'll be trapped inside the house. If we are outside, at least, we can run."

Jane looked Orla squarely in the eyes. She was much smaller than Orla, but her inner strength made Orla squirm a bit. "Why did you come here?" Jane asked with a voice as cool as water.

"I saw the shapeshifters moving in this direction. I didn't have time to get to Lorcan, so I came straight here. This is Lorcan's home, and I'll help him protect it as much as I can."

"But he left this home for you."

Orla looked straight into Jane's eyes. "We are soulmates, Jane. Without each other, our lives have no meaning. I left my family because they forbade me to love him. When you kept him from loving me, it was like asking him to refuse his life. What did you expect him to do?"

"I'm sure Lorcan has told you by now that the reason we have him is because of Bricius. When Lorcan was six, he killed one of Bricius's shapeshifters in the woods to protect me. The day he came home and told me he kissed you for the first time, he was covered in Bricius's aura . . ."

"He taught my magic class. I practiced some of his magic, and of course, it carried his aura. I have no blood ties with him."

"At that time, Keeva was a toddler. Bricius was our biggest fear. We worried that he'd come for her at any time. How do you expect I'd react when Lorcan came home with our worst nightmare?"

"You asked him not to see me again without even giving him a reason."

Jane nodded. "That was exactly what I did."

"Lorcan killed Bricius in our last mission."

"I knew that. I felt the deep wound in my soul suddenly stop bleeding. I don't know how, but I just knew that the nightmare had stopped, and Lorcan was coming home. I didn't know that Bricius would get his last strike that killed my husband."

"Yet you released the wolf so he could save Alana, a descendant of Bricius's clan?"

Jane smiled. "I will never forgive Bricius, but this is no fault of his descendants. Now he's dead. And so is Ferris. I now consider that chapter of our lives closed. Keeva and Lorcan have to move on . . . And you have to move on."

They heard a bang on the back door. "Come with me." Orla took Jane's hand and ran toward the living room. "They've start attacking already. Are the rooms upstairs secured?" Orla asked.

"Yes," Keeva said.

"Noah, can you go upstairs with Jane? Go into a room and secure all the doors. Don't open for anyone except us. Take the cat and use the fireballs if you have to. Can you do that for me?"

Noah nodded. Aris jumped onto his shoulders.

"Give me your knife," Jane said.

"Mother!" Keeva exclaimed.

"Take mine." Orla gave Jane hers.

Jane nodded and took the knife. "I'll take care of Noah." Then she rushed upstairs.

CHAPTER 38

"You have a hell of a mother, Keeva." Orla mumbled. There was more banging on the back door. Orla grabbed the captured shapeshifter and used him as a shield. She opened the front door and walked outside. All the pumas and leopards in the front hunched down, growling, preparing for an attack.

"Withdraw, or I'll set him on fire." Orla said and threw a fireball at a tree in the front yard. The tree burst into flames. "Now, withdraw!" Orla yelled at the animals. They kept growling, unsure of what to do. There were rows and rows of them. A sea of shapeshifters walked stealthily around them.

Then she heard a haunting howl, the coolest howl Orla had ever heard. "Mori!" Orla exclaimed under her breath and grinned. Beneath the moonlight, Mori appeared—a magnificent warrior with an army of space foxes. "This is the end of you!" Orla threw the shapeshifter she was holding hostage to his frontline and ran back to inside the house.

Mori and her foxes attacked the shapeshifters from behind.

From another direction, more howling came. Roy and his space wolves charged toward them. The banging from the back of the house had stopped, replaced by the groaning of wounded dogs. Lorcan and Riley stormed in from the back door.

"Your mother and Noah are upstairs!" Orla told them. They heard a thumping sound from above. Lorcan and Riley raced up the stairs. Orla turned and threw fireballs at some pumas that had gotten past Mori's foxes. Another leopard jumped for the broken window, but Keeva gunned it down instantly. Maeve and Bradan rushed toward the back door to guard it.

Lorcan arrived at the landing upstairs and was in awe. His mother had her knife held at the throat of a puma, and Noah had thrown a leopard off balance with a fireball. The animal rolled off the roof and landed outside. By the sound of it, the shapeshifter was finished off by Maeve and Bradan in the backyard.

The puma wriggled and got free from Jane's knife, and it jumped at Noah. Riley darted at the animal, aiming his rifle upward, and shot. The dead puma landed on top of Riley, sending him rolling and sliding down the stairs.

Then everything went quiet.

"We've got the outside covered at the front," Mori yelled.

"I've got the back," Roy added.

"The upstairs is fine," Lorcan said and darted down the stairs.

At the bottom of the stairs, Riley lay beneath the dead puma. Lorcan dragged the puma off his friend. Riley was lying upside down. Lorcan was worried he'd broken his neck in the fall. When he approached, Keeva pushed in front of him and gently put her hand behind Riley's neck and back. "No blood. Doesn't seem to be broken. He might have a concussion, though," she muttered more to herself than to the others in the room. Riley opened his eyes groggily.

"There you are. Give me a smile so I know you understand me," Keeva said.

Riley winced.

"That doesn't qualify as a smile, but it should do for now. I'm going to try to move you, okay? Tell me where it hurts."

"Left shoulder," Riley said.

"Welcome back, doctor." Keeva smiled.

***

Later, Lorcan and Orla saw Mori and Roy back to the portal. Bradan and Maeve helped to clean up the mess in the house. From the sofa in the living room, Lorcan heard Keeva's voice, "Don't be a puss. Stay still. I'll fix it."

"Have you done this before?" asked Riley.

"I fixed a pig's tail. He was alive and healthy."

"What about his tail?"

In another corner, Noah was sitting on a bench with Aris on his lap, enjoying the scene of Keeva playing doctor with his father.

Lorcan fixed the bandage on Orla's shoulder and kissed it. "How does it feel?" he asked.

"Better." She smiled at him. "Sorry I missed the show at the ceremony."

Lorcan chuckled. "It wasn't much of a show. Ciaran did a spectacular job with the special effects, though. The moon really looked as if it was on fire. And I don't know how the hell Riley pulled off the fake wolf fur stunt. It looked so real that Alana couldn't tell."

"I'm sure it wasn't easy. I'm sorry I left you alone to do all that."

He kissed her cheek. "That's okay. You were busy saving my family." He kissed her, but she stopped the kiss.

"Should we go and talk to your mother?"

He cringed, and Orla laughed.

CHAPTER 39

The riverbank was cold as usual. Lorcan wasn't sure that walking along this riverbank before going back to Eudaiz was a good idea. It was associated with too many painful memories. But Orla had insisted. Perhaps she valued the good memories over the daunting experiences. She wanted to remember the good times they had spent here during their childhoods and the moment they had become childhood sweethearts.

They approached the large rock where Lorcan had always hopped up first and reached his hand out to bring her up with him. He always felt good doing that. It made him feel like a prince. Recalling the experience, he chuckled.

"What?" Orla asked.

He looked at the way her long hair blew in the wind and the way she squinted her eyes when the hair tangled in her face. He did what she always expected—he untangled the hair on her face and kissed her squinting eyes, then her exquisite nose, working his way to her lips.

They heard children giggle in the distance and saw a group of families gather for a picnic. It wasn't exactly a summer picnic under the glorious sunlight. But considering this riverbank always seemed to be the territory of creatures and black magic, the scene of families gathering was quite a treasure.

Orla smiled.

"What are you smiling at?" Lorcan asked.

She looked up at him, twirled her finger in a strand of his hair, and gazed into his eyes. He loved the way she looked into his eyes, so intense, as if she was examining them, memorizing them, and savoring the moment. He knew he wanted to do the same to her, but hell, he wouldn't be able to do it as well as she did.

"I'm just happy, that's all," Orla said.

"Would you be happier seeing that?"

"What?"

Lorcan realized that with her human senses, she probably couldn't see and hear what he could. Across the river, deep in the woods, Bradan and Maeve were walking, hand in hand. He described what he saw to Orla.

"About last night, you weren't disappointed, were you?"

Orla shook her head. "No. Your mother was tired. She'd had a hell of a day."

Lorcan looked down at the sand. "Still, I'd love to see you two talk before we leave."

"No, you wouldn't. You squirmed when I suggested it."

"I did not!" Lorcan laughed as Orla punched him lightly in the chest. Then the smiled faded on Orla's face. Lorcan turned to see his mother approaching.

Jane smiled. "So you two are leaving now?"

Lorcan nodded. "We'll be back to visit you in no time."

Jane looked at Orla. "I thought it was too soon for me to come to terms with everything. Too hard to forgive and forget in such a short time. But I thought about it all night, and you were right. Life is short and precious. I have to treasure every moment of it."

Lorcan put his hand on Orla's back and rubbed it lightly. She had his support in whatever was coming.

Jane pulled out a necklace. "This belongs to my mother. I had kept it for Keeva, but now I'm giving it to you." She put it around Orla's neck. "Keeva will always have me. But you don't have anyone. You two can take care of each other. But when you are out there, I want you to know that you always have my love and my blessing."

Orla embraced Jane. Lorcan raised his hand to wipe a tear rolling down Orla's face. But the tear and the scene Orla and his mother holding each other was too beautiful for him to disturb.

He was glad they had come back to Ireland and thankful that they had worked things out. The riverbank was now at peace. He was grateful she had given him the little rock as a promise of their childhood love. He thanked the person who had created him as a supernatural creature, just so he could prove that it wasn't his creation that made him who he was; it was his mother's nurturing that had guided his emotions and made him the human he was today.

For a limited time, D.N. Leo gives away
4 books in the Multiverse Collection

CLAIM YOUR FREE E-BOOKS
http://narrativeland.com

THANK YOU FOR READING!
D.N. LEO

D.N. LEO 'S NOVELS
SERIES READING ORDER

http://narrativeland.com/dnleonovels

—

A SHADE OF MIND

(narrativeland.com/shade)
Main Characters: Ciaran, Madeline, Tadgh, and Jo
(Recommended reading in order)
1-4 Random Psychic
2-4 Forever Mortal
3-4 Elusive Beings
4-4 Imperfect Divine

—

SPECTRUM

(narrativeland.com/spectrum)
Main characters: Lorcan, Orla, Roy and Mori
(Recommended reading in order)
1-4 White Curse
2-4 Blue Fox
3-4 Indigo Stone
4-4 Red Moon

—

MINDSCAPE
(narrativeland.com/mind)
Main characters:
Ciaran, Madeline, Tadgh, Jo, Kyle, Hoyt, Ayana, Pete,
Sizx, Lorcan, Orla
(Recommended reading in order within series, can be
read in ANY order in related to other series)

Queen's Gambit
Knight & Pawn
Lone Castle
Doubled Bishops
Dead Squares
King's Endgame

—

SILVER BLOOD
Main characters:
(narrativeland.com/silver)
Ciaran, Madeline, Tadgh, Jo, Caedmon, Sedna, Roy,
Mori, Zach, Mya, Lorcan and Orla
This series can be read in ANY order within the series
and in related to other series.

Virgo
Libra
Scorpio
Taurus
Pisces
Gemini

Thank you for reading.

If you enjoyed reading **Spectrum of Lies – Book 4**, I would appreciate it if you would help others enjoy this book, too.

Recommend it. Please help other readers find this book by recommending it to friends, readers' groups and discussion boards.

Review it. Please tell other readers why you liked this book by reviewing it wherever you purchase the book from. If you do write a review, please send me an email at info@dnleo.com so I can thank you with a personal email.

COPYRIGHT

BREAK A CURSE
-RED MOON-

SPECTRUM OF LIES
BOOK 4

By D.N. Leo

Copyright © 2015 by D.N. Leo, all rights reserved.

This is a work of fiction. Any resemblance to actual business or persons is purely coincidental.

Reproduction in whole or part of this publication without express written consent from the author is strictly prohibited.

I greatly appreciate you taking the time to read my work. Please consider leaving a review wherever you purchased the book, and refer the book to your friends.

www.ingramcontent.com/pod-product-compliance
Lightning Source LLC
Chambersburg PA
CBHW060622260626
47161CB00008B/2774